parABnormal Magazine

September 2023

Edited by H. David Blalock

parABnormal Magazine
September 2023

parABnormal Magazine is a work of fiction. Names, characters, places, and incidents are products of the authors' imaginations. Any resemblance to actual events or persons, living or dead, is entirely coincidental.

Story and illustration copyrights owned by the respective authors and artists.

Cover illustration "Chlorine Slumber" by Joana Solà
Cover design by Laura Givens
First Printing, September 2023
Hiraeth Publishing
http://www.hiraethsffh.com/

Visit http://www.hiraethsffh.com/ for online science fiction, fantasy, horror, scifaiku, and more. Support the small, independent press...

Vol. V, No. 3   September 2023
parABnormal Magazine is published quarterly on the 15th day of March, June, September, and December in the United States of America by Hiraeth Publishing, P.O. Box 1248, Tularosa, NM, 88352. Copyright 2022 by Hiraeth Publishing. All rights revert to authors and artists upon publication except as noted in selected individual contracts. Nothing may be reproduced in whole or in part without written permission from the authors and artists. Any similarity between places and persons mentioned in the fiction or semi-fiction and real places or persons living or dead is coincidental. Writers and artists guidelines are available online at www.hiraethsffh.com. Guidelines are also available upon request from Hiraeth Publishing, P.O. Box 1248, Tularosa, NM, 88352, if request is accompanied by a self-addressed ***10 envelope with a first-class US stamp. Editor: H David Blalock.

Contents

Stories

Poems

Articles

*

A Little Help, Please

In the world of the small indie press we fight a never-ending battle for attention to our work, as writers and in publishing. Here's an example: big publishers [you know who they are] have gobs of $$$ that they can devote to advertising and marketing. Here at Hiraeth Publishing, our advertising budget consists of the deposits for whatever soda bottles and aluminum cans we can find alongside the highways. Anti-littering laws make our task even more difficult . . . J

That's where YOU come in. YOU are our best promoter. YOU are the one who can tell others about us. Just send 'em to our website, tell them about our store. That's all. Just that.

Of course, we don't mind if you talk us up. We're pretty good, you know. We have some award-winning and award-nominated writers and artists, plus other voices well-deserving to be heard [not everyone wins awards, right?] but our publications are read-worthy nevertheless.

That number once again is:

www.hiraethsffh.com

Friend us on Facebook at Hiraeth Publishing

Follow us on Twitter at @HiraethPublish1

What???

No subscription to parABnormal
Magazine??

We can fix that . . .

Just go here and order:

https://www.hiraethsffh.com/product-
page/parabnormal-magazine-subscription

*...also makes a great gift
any time of the year*

The Last Train to Deakin Valley
by Mike Adamson

Peter Larkin is a young photographer working for the railway press. He discovers a disused line, but struggles to find any reference to it. His search connects him with a "white witch" in the village of Hathersage, who has all the answers – she was born in the village at the end of that line, a village which no longer exists.

In 1924, a disaster occurred in the Deakin Tunnel, and a large part of the village's population died terribly in an inferno. The line was closed, the tunnel boarded up, and Deakin Valley began to die. Ever since, a "ghost train" has run on the lost line, and the sound of the train in the night has lured people to follow – and none ever return.

Peter gives in to the grim occult compulsion dragging his every thought back to the lost line. He penetrates Deakin Tunnel, only to confront the terrible forces at play...

https://www.hiraethsffh.com/product-page/last-train-to-deakin-valley

ePub:
https://www.hiraethsffh.com/product-page/the-last-train-to-deakin-valley-1

The Puppets of Low Magic
By Lorraine Pinelli Brown

The late 17th/early 18th centuries marked a time of awakening, with the birth of institutions of higher learning, yet the most enlightened of that time spent their cognitive brilliance debating how many angels could fit upon the head of a pin. Satan was ubiquitous, and he was known to have appeared in many forms. He was thought forever present on the earth, a wolf amongst God's holy sheep; watching, waiting for his chance to corrupt the faithful. Temptation loomed—witchcraft was actually practiced—and good men prayed hard for deliverance from Beelzebub and his foul minions.

Rachel Mapes is a Puritan woman who, upon accident of birth, receives an IQ of 160. She has a level of understanding that would take others years of book-learning to achieve. She is able to make connections where it would seem no connection was possible. She possesses strong powers of intuition. And she has to hide her special abilities . . . or be burned at the stake.

But what if she really *is* a witch . . . ?

Print: https://www.hiraethsffh.com/product-page/puppets-of-low-magic-by-lorraine-pinelli-brown

ePub: https://www.hiraethsffh.com/product-page/puppets-of-low-magic-by-lorraine-pinelli-brown-2

pdf: https://www.hiraethsffh.com/product-page/puppets-of-low-magic-by-lorraine-pinelli-brown-1

The Green Lady
By M. R. Williamson

You look at a grandfather's clock—and the clock looks back at you! There's a mist inside it.

You find the words "GET OUT" on the back wall of the closet. In fresh red paint! Still dripping!

A voice from the hay loft screams, "Get out!"

It's the Green Lady of Weeping Willows. What does she want? Well, open the book...

https://www.hiraethsffh.com/product-page/green-lady-by-m-r-williamson

pdf eBook: https://www.hiraethsffh.com/product-page/green-lady-by-m-r-williamson-1

ePub eBook: https://www.hiraethsffh.com/product-page/copy-of-green-lady-by-m-r-williamson

Bone Deep
Shannon Taft

It was supposed to be simple, I thought as I lay in bed, staring out the window at the winter-bare tree branches that resembled skeletal fingers in the light of the half-moon. My jaw ached, but that wasn't what had woken me up. It was the part of me that wasn't *me* causing all the trouble, and now I was terrified to close my eyes.

Only twelve hours earlier, the dental surgeon had yanked out the tooth that I'd managed to crack so deeply a crown wasn't an option. Reclining in Dr. Avilla's patient chair, I told him, "I swear, I will never again open a plastic soda bottle with my teeth."

He smirked, ruining his jolly appearance that had made me think of Santa when I'd first met him. "That's what they all say, Janelle. You'd be surprised how many other patients in their twenties I get. Sports, drunken accidents, and yes, biting down on things you shouldn't."

"I've learned my lesson."

He arched a snowy-white eyebrow. "We'll see. In the meantime, you'll have a gap for six months where the old tooth was while we wait for the bone to fill in so that I can implant the post."

I wrinkled my nose in disgust. "A hole is gonna look awful."

"The tooth was a molar. Way back there, no one will even notice. Now, if you get any granular residue in your mouth over the next few days, I want you to call us."

"Granular... Oh, no. Do not even tell me..."

"I did warn you, we use donated materials."

"Yeah, that's a nice way to say you ground up some dead guy's bones and sewed it under my gums."

Dr. Avilla's mischievous grin was more suited to an evil elf. "It'll help you grow new bone to fill in where your tooth's roots were. We need that spot nice and solid to hold the post for your new tooth. If it isn't strong enough, then when I drill—"

I held up a hand to stop him. I didn't want to think about metal posts being drilled into me, or about how someone else's bones were going to fuse with mine. But even worse would be the ground-up corpse-bone working its way out of the pocket in my gums. What if I swallowed the material? Would that make me technically a cannibal?

Only half a day later, I wished I had that problem. The cadaver material hadn't slipped out. It was still there. And its name was Bob.

***

The nightmare had begun with me looming over the corpse of a man in his forties, his hair thinning at the crown. Slouched behind the wheel of a red sports car, he wore a perfectly-tailored suit in charcoal gray and a Patek Phillipe watch. Blood was splattered on the ivory leather upholstery. A gun rested on the passenger seat, not far from his right hand.

But in the dream, I considered that dead body my own. I was Bob, and we felt so lost. *How? Why? I don't understand!*

The confusion shifted quickly to rage. *I'm Bob Parchelson! I'm too important to die like this.*

I'd woken up bathed in a fury unlike anything I've known before. As it faded and I regained my own sense of identity, I pondered the name the dead man had clung to—refusing to surrender it even once he'd been robbed of his body.

Bob Parchelson.

I was certain I'd heard that name on the radio news station a few months before. Bob had been the owner of Parchelson's Fine Furniture, a chain of stores that spanned half the country. It was reported that he'd committed suicide in the parking lot of one of our area's more isolated hiking trails.

Apparently, Bob didn't agree that it was a suicide —and he ought to know.

Of course, that assumed the nightmare had really come from Bob. I gave an uneven laugh as I pondered the odds. My imagination being in overdrive made far more sense than believing my bone donor was reaching out from the great beyond to complain about his death.

"You're an idiot," I whispered to myself. "Just go back to sleep."

Exhausted, I shut my eyes. It took a while, but I eventually managed to drift off to dreamland.

When I woke again an hour later, angrier than ever over being murdered, I said, "Okay, I'll prove this is nuts."

I reached for the iPad on my nightstand and began to search the Internet. There was surprisingly little to be found about a man as wealthy as Bob. Depending on what privacy level he'd wanted in life, he'd either had a terrible PR person or an exceptionally good one who was skilled at keeping him out of the news. But a rich man's death always draws attention.

I clicked on a newspaper report from three months earlier. It listed Bob's age, profession, where the body had been found, and that suicide was suspected. It was accompanied by a photo of Bob, sitting ramrod straight in a boardroom setting. I was certain I'd never seen his face before, other than in my dream. So, how could I have known in that vision what features he should have?

My stomach knotted as the seemingly impossible became more plausible. "Bob? You there?"

I received no reply.

Perhaps I needed to be asleep, like before, with my mind shut down, in order for him to communicate? Gnawing on a fingernail, I decided that the middle of the night was not the best time to assess the supernatural capabilities of cadaver donation substances.

"Okay, Bob," I said, restoring the iPad to my nightstand. "I'm going back to sleep now. If you're real and have anything useful to tell me, the floor is all yours."

I hoped he'd see this as a generous offer and not my acceptance of the fact that I didn't know how to stop him from invading my dreams. As I lay my head against my satin pillowcase, comforted by the lavender scent, I said, "Hey, Bob? I get that you're focused on losing your life and body, but showing me the face of your shooter might be more helpful."

I woke up two hours later, the night still dark and my head filled with a half-dozen garbled images—none from the shooting.

I tried to bring some mental order to the collection. The first vignette had Bob still in his body, standing at the altar in tux while sliding a ring onto the finger of a gorgeous blonde who looked younger than me.

It had been followed by a confusingly similar vision. Same church, same minister, same groom—different young blonde. But the minister's hair had gone heavily grey, and he'd developed wrinkles around his eyes. From that, I deduced that the ceremonies were years apart. "You traded the first wife in for a new model, Bob? No wonder you ended up dead. If—"

A stabbing pain in my jaw cut me off before I could say anything else. That Bob was real enough to do it was even more awful than the pain.

My voice trembled as I said, "Got it, Bob. I won't critique your life choices."

He must've taken me at my word, because the pain receded to a dull throb.

The images I'd seen were fading, and I still had several more to process. I scrambled for my tablet, opened the notes app, and described each scene as best I could, speaking as I typed. "Bob in a warehouse arguing with a guy two inches shorter. Bob flushed with rage, guy cowering."

I managed not to articulate my views on bosses who were bullies, but the throbbing in my jaw increased. "You reading my mind, Bob?"

The sensation turned to a sharp thrust, then disappeared entirely.

"Okay. As much as I don't want that again, let's do a little test." I clenched my hands into fists as I thought, *Bob, do one quick jolt if you hear me.*

Agony spread from the vicinity of my missing molar, only to dissipate in a scant second. My life's experience with physical pain had mostly been the stubbed-toe variety, but I'd never experienced any kind that came with an off-switch.

"Test successful," I told Bob. As soon as the words were out of my mouth, I wondered if I'd been unwise to confirm for him how much power he had. "Let's get back to what you showed me. There were two wives, someone you were mad at in a warehouse..." I felt my brow furrow as I tried to remember more.

"Did I see you taking some furniture apart in another room?" There was no objection from my jaw, so I entered it into my tablet. As best as I recalled, it was a place with brick walls and a concrete floor, and he'd been applying a crowbar to a four-inch-thick slab of walnut that formed the top of a dining room table.

15

"I like this no-pain thing better, Bob. Let's reserve stomping on my nerve endings for when I get it wrong. I think I also saw you, pen in hand, in some fancy office, reading a document that started by promising you were of sound mind." I wished I could make the same claim at that moment. "So, you were signing a will?"

The tranquility in my jaw implied that he was.

"Did you cut out your newest wife?"

That got me a stab of pain. "There's a no." I ran down a list of common relatives that most people have. Son, daughter, mom, dad, sister, brother... Just when I was ready to quit to escape the punishment, I said, "Nephew."

My molar space was blissfully numb.

"Got it. Disinherited nephew." I added it to the notes, then realized what was missing. "You didn't show me the shooting. I'm gonna assume that means you don't remember it."

Bob didn't disagree, and I wondered what else he might not recall that we could've found useful.

I jotted down everything else I could remember from the dreams. By the time I was done, the sky was turning shades of pink and purple, like a neon bruise.

"I'm in no condition to teach a bunch of five year olds like this," I muttered, rubbing my left jaw, even though Bob hadn't walloped me in a while. "But the school getting a substitute at the last minute—"

The ache came back. I suspected that Bob was saying he wanted my time spent purely on finding his killer. I felt committed too, despite my resentment over a lost night of sleep and intermittent nerve agony. If children aren't allowed to steal each other's toys, then adults shouldn't get to steal each other's lives.

Plus, I didn't want an angry murder victim

16

lurking around in my body. Bob needed closure, or at the very least, some peace if I was to have any.

I reached for my phone and called in sick, citing incapacitation from my oral surgery. I opted not to mention the nature of the incapacity, as I preferred to be employed when this was all over. I also sent my team leader a text about the location of my sub packet, stuffed full of exercises to keep the kids entertained—or so I hoped.

Work taken care of, Bob and I got back to suspect hunting. I wanted a name for the warehouse guy, so I reopened my tablet and scavenged around in the bowels of the Parchelson's Fine Furniture website looking for an employee roster. When I stumbled upon an org chart, I said, "Tell me if I find him," then read aloud every name I could find. Bob left me alone until I reached the name of his vice-president for purchasing, Geoffrey Scharf.

I added it to the notes.

As for the nephew, I didn't know where to look for his name. I was ready to give up on that when it occurred to me to just go through the alphabet letter-by-letter. I sang my way through it—slightly off-pitch —over and over until we'd spelled out Q-u-e-n-t-i-n.

I repeated the process for Bob's current and former wives.

"We're doing good, Bob," I said, scrolling through my notations. "Now, if anyone here should be removed from candidacy, let me know. Your ex-wife, Althea. Current wife, Suzanne. Disinherited nephew, Quentin. Employee, Geoffrey Scharf."

Bob expressed no objection to my suspects.

"Anyone else?"

There was a pause, then a dull ache. The delay confused me, as did the weakness of the message.

"Give me a quick ping if that was your way to say you're not sure."

The pain was sharp and brief.

"Got it. I'll keep an open mind. But let's start with the names we've got. The question is how to find out more about these people." I opened Bob's obituary. It said he had twin sons who were a year old, but listed no other children. "You were forty-seven when you died. I'm twenty-six myself. Were you frisky in college —maybe some drunken sex you barely recalled in the morning?"

I got a piercing jolt for saying that.

"Was that you being insulted, or saying no? Let's do this, if you were just being defensive, or mean to the innocent kindergarten teacher who's trying to help you, send a dull throb."

On cue, the throb arrived. It was so soft that I took it for an apology.

"Okay, send no pain if it is plausible that your activities—whatever they were—could've resulted in a secret daughter. One that you didn't tell people about."

My jaw stayed peaceful.

"If I claim to be her, and that before you died you told me a bunch of stuff about you, your family, and your business, would these people find it believable?"

No pain.

"It seems we have a plan to explain my involvement." I grinned in relief. "Now, let's perfect my spiel. I need to be able to tell your lawyer stuff that a stranger couldn't know in order to get them on our side."

We worked on my script for half an hour with me guessing things at random and making a list of the ones that Bob said were true. When we were done, I used the internet to track down the name of Bob's law firm, then ran down the list of lawyers on the firm's website until Bob signaled that I'd reached the correct one: Mike Chutes.

I called but got voicemail, so I left a message. "Mr. Chutes, my name is Janelle Wilcox. Um..." I forgot my next line and lowered my head to read the script I'd prepared. "I'm Bob Parchelson's daughter. He told me to call you if anything happened to him. I'm sorry I didn't do this sooner. I was scared. He didn't commit suicide, you see. He warned me that someone might try to kill him. Please call me back as soon as you can." I recited my telephone number and hung up.

It didn't take long for the phone to ring. Mike Chutes had a comforting baritone voice, but he sounded skeptical as he said, "Explain to me again who you are?"

I went through a variation of my script, then the lawyer pelted me with questions. Thanks to some help from Bob, I navigated the minefields. As soon as I could, I moved the conversation to the list of suspects.

When I said the word "nephew," Mike snarled, "I *knew* Quentin was a little creep." That's when I finally felt like we had the lawyer on our side; but I wished I'd known that Quentin's name would be so easy to get. All that running through the alphabet, and Mike had said the name before I even could.

I explained to Mike that I wanted to meet the people from my list to see if, by working together, we could solve the murder. "Between what Bob has told me, plus what they each know, we might catch someone in a lie. Can you find an excuse to bring them together?"

"I can probably get most of them," Mike said slowly. "We're still working on probate, and if I tell them something's gone wrong and they need to come in, they will. Scharf will be a little harder, but I think I can come up with an excuse. However..." His voice grew more resolute when he continued, "I have a responsibility to my client, even if he is dead. I need to notify the police that it might not have been a suicide."

I pondered the pros and cons of involving law enforcement, including the risk that they'd find out I was lying about being Bob's daughter. When the silence had gone on too long, Mike said, "Ms. Wilcox?"

Time was up, so I went with my best guess on the right way to handle things. "I'd feel safer with a cop around for the meeting, so if you invite one to be in the room next door, I'm fine with you telling them it's because Bob might've been murdered. But can you please not mention me, specifically, just yet? If the killer finds out about my existence, I could be in danger."

The desperation in my voice wasn't only caused by my fears of being hunted by a murderer. I didn't know how long Bob could stick around once our bones started to fuse, and while I hoped he'd be gone soon, I needed him to help me question the suspects. "I'd like the meeting done as soon as possible, before anything can go wrong."

"I understand your concerns," Mike said, even though he couldn't possibly comprehend my real situation. "Now, about you being Bob's daughter. His will—"

"I know I'm not named in there," I interjected, wanting to assure him that this wasn't a scam to get money. "And I'm not going to make a fuss about being left out of his estate. All I want is justice for his murder."

Bob sent me a ping of raw nerve endings that made no sense to me. Pain was a crappy way for him to thank me for trying to catch his killer.

A sigh carried through the phone before Mike said, "We can discuss the will some other time."

Shortly after lunch, Mike sent me a text saying that things were set for his office at five that evening. It was much faster than I'd been daring to hope. "Benefit of you being able to afford the best lawyers, right, Bob?"

I dressed in a black suit with a white blouse—my "parent-teacher meeting" uniform— and took the Metro to get to Mike's office. The law firm took up the entire top floor of a fifteen-story building. Having aimed to get there a half-hour early, I managed to arrive only eight minutes late.

The lobby had a surfeit of glossy cherrywood furniture, and I wondered if they'd purchased it from Bob. There were also four burgundy leather couches. A man in his mid-fifties wearing a three-piece suit, with salt-and-pepper hair and an improbable tan, stood near the reception desk alongside a guy in his thirties wearing business-casual slacks, a navy oxford shirt, and a gun. The armed man's stance said "police" as loudly as any badge would've.

No one else was around.

"I'm Mike Chutes," the older man said, holding out a hand for me to shake. "This is Detective Woodbury."

Glancing around the cavernous lobby, I saw no one else and assumed that Bob's nearest and dearest had been stashed in a conference room. "Janelle Wilcox. Am I the last to arrive?"

"I only invited one of the people you asked for," Mike admitted with a small wince.

Bob expressed his displeasure at the news by stabbing me in the mandible. It seemed unfair, since he was the one who'd hired an unreliable attorney. "Mister Chutes, we agreed you would—"

Detective Woodbury cut me off. "He notified the police about you and your plan, as was his duty. I told him not to arrange the meeting you requested."

I shot Mike a glare.

He gave me an unrepentant, bland stare in return. "Bob was my client, Ms. Wilcox. Not you. His interests come first, and I never promised to keep you a secret. I only said I understood your position."

"Lawyers," I muttered.

The detective, who probably comprehended only too well the headache of dealing with attorneys, grinned for a second before getting his face under control. "After speaking to Mister Chutes, we checked with Parchelson's first wife, Althea. She was his college girlfriend and we hoped she might know if there was merit to your story about being his child."

I was astonished they'd take her word for a thing like that. "He never told her about me, detective."

"She said that your name was unfamiliar. Your mother's name was equally unknown to her."

I pictured the many ways the police might've discovered my mom's name and prayed that they hadn't contacted her to ask if she'd ever dated Bob. She'd probably have told them she'd never heard of the man.

Was I about to be arrested for fraud? Hoping that Bob's mind reading abilities were intact, I silently scolded, "This is all your fault! All I did was open a freaking soda bottle with my teeth, and I got stuck with you!"

Something might have shown on my face, because Woodbury asked, "Is something wrong?"

"Sore tooth," I replied.

"Yes, well..." Woodbury looked unconvinced. "As it happens, we were initially under the impression that Bob Parchelson might've committed suicide because he was about to be implicated in drug smuggling."

It took me a second to process that, after which, I shouted much too loudly, "The table!" My voice was more moderate when I added, "Bob figured out someone was up to no good and found the stuff in a walnut table."

I assumed that had to be why he'd been going at it with a crowbar and why he'd shared the image with me. When Bob lodged no objection to my statement, I was sure I had it right.

Woodbury gave me a piercing stare. "Inside a *walnut* table? We checked the warehouse and inventory lists for any furniture where someone might hide substantial drugs. None of the cabinets or end tables with drawers were walnut—not within the last year."

I was sure the table had to be important for Bob to show it to me. Perhaps I'd guessed the wood type wrong, or maybe it had been labeled differently on the official inventory records? "It was a dining-room table, about four-inches thick on the top." I held my thumb and index finger that distance apart to demonstrate. "I guess the smugglers hollowed it out or something. Bob had a crowbar, so it's probably not easy to break open."

Woodbury suddenly grinned like a boy with a new video game. He pulled out his phone and called someone. A few seconds later he said, "Yeah, it's me. You have the list of which furniture she got from Parchelson's? Great. Look for a dining-room table."

We all stood around in silence for at least half a minute, the detective shifting from foot to foot with eager anticipation—that, or he needed a restroom. Then he froze for a moment before saying to the person on the phone, "Perfect. Make sure we include the dining-room table in the warrant request. We're gonna want to get that thing x-rayed at the lab."

Whose dining-room had that table? I remembered Bob attacking it in a place with brick walls and concrete floors—not a fancy home. To me, that meant

23

the furniture wasn't his wife's, or he wouldn't have needed to open it in a warehouse.

When Woodbury got off the phone, I tested my theory. "How did you know to ask about Althea's furniture?"

"We have you to thank for that. The DEA had a tap on Scharf's phone for the smuggling investigation, to see if he was involved. As soon as I got off the phone with Althea this morning, she called Scharf. Apparently, they cooked up the smuggling after Parchelson divorced her. They were so occupied with discussing why you were coming out of nowhere that they were careless discussing their whole situation, including the murder and smuggling operation."

"Then why don't you arrest them?" I pleaded.

Woodbury raised his eyebrows. It felt like a scolding for my impertinence. His tone was professionally cool as he said, "Ordinarily, we'd have waited to see if we could get additional incriminating statements, or even catch them in the same room as the drugs. But Scharf already had plans to leave the country next week on a buying trip, and thanks to your unexpected arrival on the scene, they decided to move that up, with her joining him. So, the DEA went ahead with the arrests." His voice grew more eager as he added, "But juries love stuff like getting to see a hidden-compartment table, and any drug residue we find inside will help back up what was said in the recording. I think we're going to do well in court."

I grinned so wide that I felt like an idiot.

Woodbury said, "Mister Chutes explained that you didn't contact us sooner because you were scared. But we have the confessions from your father's killers—and know about that table—only because you were brave enough to come forward. I imagine your father would be very proud of you." He

24

took a business card from his pocket and held it out towards me. "If you have any questions, please feel free to call me."

"Thank you. Bob thanks you—I mean would thank you—too."

"You're very welcome," Woodbury said before departing.

As the elevator doors closed behind him, I slid the card into my pocket, then turned to Mike and said, "Thanks for bringing the detective—and for ignoring my request that you invite the others here."

"Woodbury isn't the person I was referring to when I said that one of your requested guests was here. Suzanne asked to meet you."

"Suzanne?" I repeated, stalling as I tried to figure out how to avoid that encounter.

"Bob's widow. She's waiting in my office. She wants to make you an offer."

"An offer?" The words were out before I realized that I was starting to sound like a parrot.

"Bob's will divides his estate equally between his wife and children. It doesn't specify the names of the children. So, if you are Bob's daughter, you're entitled to a quarter of the estate."

Was this what Bob had been trying to tell me by stomping on my nerve endings when the will came up before? Queasy at the notion that I'd accidentally started the process of defrauding Bob's widow and children, I stumbled over to a burgundy sofa. As much as I wanted to tell Mike that he could forget about me being an heir, I didn't know how to explain doing that. Was I going to have to make these people go through the farce of a DNA test?

A thought occurred to me, and I stopped breathing for a second. What if Bob's donor material lurking in my mandible affected the DNA results?

At the very least, I ought to avoid any mouth

swabs.

Suddenly, a voice said from the hallway in a thick French accent, "I'll offer you ten percent now."

I looked up to see a willowy blonde with a tissue clenched in her fist. It was the bride from the more recent of Bob's weddings. "Ma'am, that's very generous, but—"

"I want to put all this behind me and return home to Marseilles." Her cerulean blue eyes shone with unshed tears.

"If I'm not Bob's daughter, I don't have a right to any of it," I said gently.

"You were still someone he trusted with the truth, when he did not trust me."

Bob responded with a sharp sting in my jaw, which I took as an instruction to speak. "I'm sure it wasn't about trust. He cared for you very much."

Suzanne shook her head, the tears slipping free.

When the silence went on, Bob prodded me again.

"He wanted to protect you from the ugliness with the suspected smuggling at his company," I said, making a guess. "As for me... He knew I might not be his and didn't want to bother you with the possibility until the facts were in. You don't owe me any money. Not even if the DNA test says Bob and I have genes in common."

Suzanne gave me a luminous smile and dabbed at her eyes with the tissue. "That's very kind of you. But if you are his, you deserve a share. And if you are not... thank you for getting justice for my Bob. For making it so my sons can grow up knowing that their father did not choose to leave them. I want you to take the ten percent either way."

"That's not necessary."

Bob suddenly stomping on my nerve endings implied disagreement. If they both wanted me to have some money, then why not accept a small token of appreciation? "Let's say only five percent, okay?"

"*Cinq million*," Suzanne said approvingly in her lilting accent.

"No, five *percent*," I corrected, certain that million meant the same thing in both languages.

She cocked her head, frowned, and turned to Mike.

He grinned at me. "In Bob's estate, five million dollars *is* five percent."

The spot in my jaw where Bob had been lurking didn't send any reply. But if silence could be smug, Bob pulled it off.

As much as I appreciated the money, that night Bob showed his gratitude in an even more important way. He sent me only one dream. We were holding his two sons in our arms on the day they were born. I woke up well rested and smiling.

I never heard from Bob again.

When you go to bed, don't leave bread or milk on the table: it attracts the dead.

— Rainer Maria Rilke, 1875-1926, Czech-German poet

From The Rim Of The Quarry
John Grey

I look down at bustling workers,
hardy men loading wagons with heavy stones,
horses straining every muscle
as they pull wagons up the rough incline,
edging forward, slipping back.

But you see only the watery remains
of a long excavation,
a sickly lime-green pond where,
years before, a young girl drowned.
Your face pales at her panic.
Your heart near breaks from the pitiable
screams.

What a couple we make -
the historian and the medium.

Hello, It's Patrick
Joseph Charles Walter

Harold brought home the green rotary-dial phone one weekday afternoon from work. It was one of the many trinkets he snagged from his job at the local Goodwill, a place we both frequented before he finally filled out an application and obtained the position of day shift cashier. Our modest two bedroom apartment was furnished with such unique and vintage items including a mound of VHS tapes, their playing devices connected to clunky televisions whose images were diseased with lines of static, a full deck of Tarot cards illustrated by an Italian artist known mysteriously as Bongo, maps of the South Georgia swamps where we were both finishing up school, and candles that had been marked half off because they were only two thirds as tall as they should have been. Harold, Harry to those closest and dearest to him, would interpret my future on rainy evenings when we forgot to pay the light bill, claiming the candles still had the power of those who had first lit their wicks.

I didn't have the heart to tell my friend I did not believe in such apparitions. Can you believe he thought I was the weird one? We both attended a regional university with thousands of fellow students, and yet he was my only true friend. My education was funded from scholarships and grants; I had never worked a day in my life, got along well with my parents, and, while Harry expected to struggle until his eventual death, I was convinced my life would be free of the chronic anxiety and existential fright he frequently spoke of.

All of this before the phone.

"We won't have to pay for phone plans anymore," Harry said. He often got caught up in the excitement of discoveries and failed to see the absence of practicality. It was a game to him – I won't bore you with all the times I had to point out the obvious flaws and lack of foresight. It was the main reason he never excelled in his studies as I did.

"But what are we going to do when we're outside the apartment? This is Valdosta. There's *murder* out there."

I thought he was going to cry. The coals in his eyes went out.

But that didn't stop him from finding the phone jack in our living room. Our complex was several decades old and each compartment was landline friendly. He had gone through with another of his ideas. He was grinning from ear to ear when I came out of my room for a bowl of oatmeal.

"It'll be fun," he said. "Let's give it a try."

So we did.

***

I had known Harry for three years until that point, ever since we had met in the upper class dormitory known as Centennial Hall. We were both in our mid-twenties, starting college late because we had reached a dead point in our lives. We were old by university standards, hence how we got stuck in Centennial. None of the girls, such pleasant creatures to gaze upon, found us attractive. We stuck out like orange thumbs.

I could easily see that my friend was the depressive type. An orphan since the age of twelve, he had been unable to find suitable employment upon reaching the legal age of adulthood despite strong marks in mathematics and the natural sciences. He found no passion in his strong drawing ability. One of the priests in the Catholic orphanage he grew up in had gifted him with a Fender guitar for his fourteenth birthday and given him two lessons a week. He clearly showed skill for anything with strings, but to him it was all technical mastery; he had no love of music.

Harold never spoke of his family, or of how they died. From what little I was able to uncover about his background, usually after we had consumed a few drinks, the parish allowed him to stay on as a ward in exchange for a handful of chores. He earned his keep by sweeping the floor and scrubbing pews. The hardest part, he said, was pretending he had faith when his heart was empty.

I guess he couldn't go on living a lie. Who am I to judge?

The first thing he did when he was hired at Goodwill was purchase a bundle of photographs. They were pictures of random people, some of them portraits that cost a nickel, others Polaroids for a penny apiece. Birthday parties, barbecues, bar mitzvahs, even a glossy printout of a human face with a skeleton for a body. At first he kept them in his room. Then, one day after class, I came home to find them framed in various positions around the apartment.

"This is my family," he said.

The collection only got bigger. I adopted them as my own relatives: we gave them names and histories, and spoke of them as if they merely resided out of state. They were our favorite aunts and grandmothers and our cousins who were backpacking through Africa. The one rule Harry seemed to have is he never framed pictures of children. Maybe they reminded him of how lonely his own adolescence had been.

I often wondered why anyone would donate packets of photos to a thrift shop. I thought that maybe it was because all these people had been abandoned by their own families for one reason or another and had been cast away like Harry had from the orphanage.

Turns out I was right.

***

It didn't ring often, but when it did it rang loud, like a locomotive screeching down the tracks. It never occurred to us that we needed to set up a number. We had been spoiled by WiFi and digital technology. I didn't even know what was making the sound the first time it happened.

DDDrrrrriiiiingggg!

It was bad the first time, worse the second. I thought it might be an alarm that the complex was on fire. I looked around expecting to see flames from the kitchen stove but everything was as it should be.

"Are you going to get that?" my friend asked.

The phone, I realized. It was lying on the beige carpet beside one of our television sets. It rang again, vibrating with each auditory emission. A shiver went through my thin frame; I don't think I have ever experienced such a moment of intense anxiety as I did during that first call, not even five years later as I watched my wife give birth to our first child.

"It's your phone," I said. "You get it."

"You're closer."

I walked over to our newest addition and picked up the handset, put it to my ear, and tilted it slightly so my lips were in front of the mouthpiece. There was a thin drizzle of static, and I immediately considered placing it back on its plastic hook, but told myself whomever was trying to reach us would just call back. With trepidation I said the word everyone musters when answering an unknown caller: "Hello."

Silence.

I was close to ending the call when finally my greeting was answered.

"Is this Patrick?" It was the voice of an elderly woman who had smoked Pall Malls her entire adult

32

life, like each syllable was its own cough.

"Speaking."

"It's Aunt Kaitlyn, baby. How are you doing?"

I had no Aunt Kaitlyn, not that I knew of anyway. But I came from a long line of Johnsons and Bermans and even a few McCutchens. She could easily have gotten lost in the family game of musical chairs.

I decided on politeness over caution. "I'm well," I said, looking over to Harry and giving him an exaggerated shrug.

"I know I missed your birthday, sweetie. I wanted you to know I put something in the mail. It's on its way from Atlanta, so it should get to you later this week." All this in between two coughing fits.

"Oh ... thank you."

There was an intake of inhalation. I imagined a wrinkled and papery oyster-like creature with an oxygen tube in its center.

"I know you have a lot of studying to do, so blow your favorite auntie a kiss."

Thankfully she hung up before I could perform any such aberration.

"Who was it?" Harry asked.

"Aunt Kaitlyn," I said.

"Your aunt in Atlanta?"

"Yeah," I said, wondering how he could have known. I wondered if I had been drinking too much.

An envelope came in the mail two days later. Aunt Kaitlyn's name was tucked into the upper left corner, her Fulton County address written below it. Inside was a card of Scooby Doo and the Gang. Also, a crisp one hundred dollar bill.

I split the money with Harry. It seemed like the right thing to do. After all, I still wasn't convinced I had actually met Aunt Kaitlyn.

***

It was one of the nights we had forgotten to keep up with the light bill. I had cooked a hasty dinner of red beans and rice over our gas stove. We couldn't open the refrigerator, so we were forced to drink tap water — not the best option in Valdosta.

It rang.

I wanted to crush the chunk of plastic with my shoe, but Harry was quick to answer, curling the cord around his fingers as he gabbed.

"Oh, hello Barry. Oh, are you? Absolutely!"

I had never heard my friend so merry. It was as if he had swallowed a particularly potent dose of cough syrup and chased it with a beer.

"I'm sure he won't mind. I'll ask him." He looked at me and said, "Do you mind if Barry comes over for a bit? His girlfriend just broke up with him."

Who was Barry? I had no idea. We never had company; even Harry preferred to meet his study partners in the campus library rather than inviting them into the apartment. We only kept things tidy out of habit.

"Not at all," I said. "I'll see if we have any booze."

"He prefers whiskey," Harry said, placing the phone back in its cradle.

I thought we had a bottle of Jim Beam in the cupboard. I left the couch to check. The bottle was mostly full and I held it in my hands as the doorbell rang. It was mild in contrast to the godawful intrusion of the rotary-dial phone. I wondered how Barry could have gotten here so fast before it dawned on me he must have already been outside and calling from his cell. Not everyone lived in the Stone Age like we did.

Now I just had to secure three glasses. I walked to the other side of the kitchen, heard the front door open, and the pleasant exchange of greetings between Harry and who I perceived to be a young man close to

34

our age.

"Cousin!"

"Cousin!"

"I had no idea you were in a relationship," Harry's voice echoed to me. I walked the path back to the living area. I had been right about Barry: he was a small, freckled young man in his mid-twenties who bore an uncanny resemblance to Harold. His hair was blonde, but it could have been a dye job.

"Patrick, have you met my cousin Barry from downtown?"

He knew I hadn't. He had told me he had no family. Surely he would have mentioned a cousin, even a distant one, who lived so nearby.

"No, I haven't."

"Well, now you have. Let's all have a seat."

He spoke with such cheer. His usual melancholy, mild-mannered self had been replaced with a glowing exuberance. I wondered if this was how he had been forced to behave in church.

I passed the bottle of Tennessee bourbon around so we could each pour our own glass. I couldn't help but notice we each took a generous offering. Unused to such strong liquor, I coughed and sputtered on the first swallow. Fortunately nobody laughed.

The conversation was a candid one. Harry's excitement grew with each sip of whiskey. I mostly rested on the couch and took it all in, pleased to see my friend in such high spirits. The bourbon brought with it a pleasant buzzing sensation, and Harry's omission of a cousin began to make more sense. As it turned out, Barry was not very likable: he was crude, spoiled, dirty behind the ears, and had an annoying habit of spitting his saliva when pronouncing anything beginning with the letter "F."

"Would you mind getting me another glass?" he asked at one point in their discussion. He was speaking to me directly, as if I were a common servant meant to gather things for him and his family.

"I have to go to the bathroom," he continued. He slid his glass across the coffee table to a spot I could barely reach, got up, and proceeded to walk down the hallway. I prayed he wasn't as careless with his pecker as he was with his tongue.

I opened the cupboard in the kitchen and selected the ugliest glass we owned, a wretched thing that had been another of Harold's contributions from his job at Goodwill. If this did not suffice, then they could take their drinking elsewhere. Or, better yet, I would call it an early night and seek solitude in my room. I still had a few chapters to read before a test in the coming week.

I continued into the living room to excuse myself, when I discovered Harry and Barry talking amongst themselves in front of several of our framed strangers. For reasons I am still not certain of to this day, I hid in the shadows of our laundry area and listened to them talk. Their voices were slightly elevated due to the effects of Jim Beam.

"Aunt Violet just moved to Kentucky. You should see her now. She is *huuuge*." Barry's voice, which I was beginning to despise. I could see why his girlfriend – any girlfriend – had broken up with him.

"And Daffodil?"

"Still living with her. She's never going to get out of that house. I keep telling her she would make an excellent attorney if only she went back to law school, but apparently she's content with living life as a data entry clerk."

"Watch it, cousin. You know I'm a mere thrift store cashier."

"Yes, but you strive for so much more. I've always envied your zeal for knowledge. You're so unlike those artsy types who waste money on a degree you can blow your nose with."

"Anyway, back to relations. Tell me about Zachery." Harold had selected the portrait of a sailor in blue camouflage.

"Not right since he got back from Afghanistan. They say the Navy's pretty easy, so I think he's buffing things up a bit for the disability pay. We come from such a terrible line of liars, don't you think?"

Harry paused for a moment before saying: "It's funny. I haven't thought of these people in such a very long time."

I hid further back as the pair (I think of us all as boys now — we were so young then) went through several of the photographs we had framed many weeks ago. Barry spoke as if he had taken supper with them just the other day.

I never gave my roommate's cousin his requested glass. He never came asking for it, either.

I almost made it to my room before something caught the corner of my eye. A photograph, a tiny one framed on the hallway wall, showed a small, freckled boy maybe ten years of age. His freckles were in the exact same pattern as the cousin in the room next to me. You could have found the North Star in that complexion.

I laid in bed and wondered what that rotary-dial phone had brought into our lives, and how Harry could be persuaded to get rid of it. I was still turning the matter over when I finally fell asleep.

***

Barry never found his way into our home again, but several others did over the next two months. They were of various ages and occupations – an elderly doctor and a thirty-something female whose beauty was so astonishing she could easily have made a career from fashion modeling for example –

37

and each seemed to have a history with my roommate. Our friendship became strained. He had guests over every night and our usual traditions were forgotten.

And the pictures in our apartment ... after each guest left, sometimes the morning after their visit, I would scour the rooms and find their faces looking back at me. They were oftentimes different ages, yet all could be identified. I even snuck inside Harold's room on occasion to find an image of the person I had been briefly introduced to the night before.

I didn't know what bothered me more: the fact that the number of pictures seemed to be growing in each room or that none of the faces were smiling. They all had distant, blank expressions, like they had just woken from a macabre dream.

Then, one evening after work, he came home excited to see me.

"Patrick, you won't believe what I have uncovered!"

He hadn't used that voice with me in quite some time. It was the tone of discovery.

"What, Harold?" I had begun using his birth name in lieu of Harry, yet another sign of our deteriorating friendship.

"We're related!"

Only then did I see the document he was holding. He presented it to me with trembling hands. The print depicted first and last names connected by short lines, beginning with his own. It was a family tree; we had learned to make them in an anthropology class we had taken together during freshman year. At the bottom of the paper, highlighted in red type, were my first, middle, and last names.

"Harold, that's crazy. If we were related, I would

know. My family reunion has over a hundred in attendance every year."

"But it's all right here. Third cousins. And to think we had been but friends this whole time!"

"Where did you get this data?" I asked, but it was more of a demand.

The annoyance in my voice did not go unnoticed.

"Patrick, I thought you would be excited. Don't you see? This means you get to use it again."

"Use what?"

"The phone! I've been wondering why it rang for you the first time. Now we know!"

I looked at the green rotary-dial device. I had forgotten that I had been the first person it had summoned. All the subsequent calls had been for Harold.

"Harold, I don't know how to tell you this ..."

"What is it?"

It was time for us to part ways. I was moving out. Goodbye, see you later.

But no. I couldn't. Harold was going crazy, and that meant he needed me more than ever. We were still friends despite the bizarre circumstances surrounding us.

I couldn't think of what to say. Should I tell him I had grown weary of his company and the presence of his "family?" I had struggled with compatibility my entire life, had called so few people friends in my twenty-five years of existence, and here I was pushing one away.

Or was it really him pushing me away?

"Go ahead, Patrick. Call someone."

"What?"

"You heard me. Call someone. You're part of the family now."

"Harold, I don't have anyone to call. This is all —"
DDDrrrrriiiiinggg!

It was like a drill to my eardrums. I wanted to crush my head into the drywall as a tinnitus sufferer must feel upon learning they will be cursed with incessant ringing for the remainder of their life. I waited, ring after terrible ring, for Harold to pick up the monstrous green instrument. Only after looking convinced I was going to vomit on our freshly vacuumed carpet did he do the service for me.

He didn't even say hello. There were a few seconds of silence before he held the receiver out to me.

"Patrick, it's for you. It's Eliza."

"I don't know anyone named Eliza."

"Of course you do! Eliza from Tuscaloosa, Alabama. She's your step-sister, for Chrissakes!"

Eliza was such an unusual name, like Beatrix or Zooey. I would have recalled a name like that. Not to mention my parents were still happily married up in Clayton County. My only sibling, an older brother ten years elder to me, was blood related.

Much to my surprise, however, I found myself taking the phone from the person I had once trusted the most. I think I was fearful of him putting it back on the hook and hearing it ring again. I didn't want to hear that dreaded noise again — not then, not ever.

"Hello, this is Patrick."

"Patrick, it's me! I came all the way 'cross state to see you. Open the door, silly!"

I wanted it to stop. I had to prove Harold wrong. I had to show him this wasn't my family.

So what did I do?

I opened the door.

***

Though I only met Eliza once, I will never forget her face. It was the shade of brown only an Alabama sun can create and devoid of any makeup that would tarnish her natural beauty. Thick chestnut colored hair fell to the middle of her back, each strand snaking into a curl. She was of average height and a little on the cuddly side, though nobody could accuse her of being fat. We were polar opposites in many ways: me being gaunt and pale and oftentimes mistaken for European whereas she was a stereotypical Southern Belle.

"Aren't you going to invite me in, Pattycake?" Her voice had a Southern twang like the inside of her mouth was coated with maple syrup.

I stepped aside so she could enter. She gave me a quick peck on the cheek, nodded to Harold, and skipped from room to room, glancing at the photographs that had become so familiar to me.

"Here I am," she said, bending over the piano case. "I didn't think you would feature me so prominently. Bryer family reunion 2015. I won the sack race."

I remembered no such event, but before I could point this out to her, Harold was bringing in drinks. The power was back on, so he had been able to secure three cold bottles of Budweiser.

"Aren't you going to ask your guest to have a seat?" he asked.

I nodded toward the couch.

"School is so *hard*. I never thought I would get into the University of Alabama. I've been thinking of going to Valdosta State with you and ...?"

"Harry," my friend said, gulping half his beer in one hearty swallow.

"And now they tell me I have to choose a major? Patrick, big brother, I don't know what I'm going to do. I've thought of taking history courses like you, but I don't want to learn all that Yankee Doodle crap first."

"Have you considered theater?" I said weakly.

"Oh, you silly nilly, don't think I haven't thought

of that. Could you really see me as an actress?"

That's exactly what you're doing, I thought. My mind hadn't gone to mud like Harold's had. Harold, who hadn't had real family since being orphaned, had been eager to accept strangers into his life. I wasn't so keen on the idea. I had even made several phone calls (on my cell, of course) to my parents three hours north to make sure they were alive and well and remembered I was their son. They were, much to my relief, enjoying the start of their retirement. I would have gone to visit them if not for the looming exams I was scheduled to take in three weeks time.

Eliza liked to talk more than listen. I learned all about my alleged relatives and their lives across the South. Eventually she got to the cousins Harold had been meeting so eagerly. Apparently our family was more than well off financially; nothing bad ever seemed to happen to anyone, although her own life was one dramatic disaster after another.

She talked well into the night. I tried not to drink too much so as to stay alert in case she slipped up and I could prove we were complete strangers to one another. The empty bottles began to accumulate, however, and eventually I couldn't count how many were mine. I was drunk.

So drunk that I let her sleep in my bed while I slept on the couch.

In the morning she was gone.

***

My academics began to suffer.

It was a week before exams and I was in no condition to study. The phone was ringing several times a day, and most of the calls were for me. Harold and I met several relatives. I dismissed my guests as soon as possible, but Harold wanted his to stay multiple nights, and I had the feeling he was going to ask some of them to move in.

I decided to move back in with my parents after the semester was over. I would take my exams, fail, then return to school later in the year. If it meant going back to Centennial, then so be it. I needed to get Harold out of my life.

I had almost settled on this decision when a new idea began to form. If it came to fruition, it just might work. I couldn't believe it had taken so long to conjure.

All it would take was one trip to Goodwill.

***

The Goodwill was on the east side of town, where there were probably more drug dealers and assailants than customers. Valdosta, while a much safer city to reside in than the belly of Atlanta, still has its rough patches, and thrift stores attract more than the charitable.

My roommate was still working the day shift, so I decided upon the evening to make my visit. It took a dreaded hour and a half to walk across town, and the idea was still a long shot, but I had no other choice. I certainly wasn't going to ask anyone in the apartment for a ride.

The inside of Goodwill was humble and musty and smelled like a basement. It housed several departments, from shoes to toddler toys. Not knowing where to look, and terrified I would be recognized if I asked an employee, I walked the aisles, browsing the shelves for what I had come for.

I found it at the very back of the store on an endcap of knick knacks. This was where we had purchased the peach scented candles we would light on nights when it seemed the sun would never dawn.

The store was closing soon, so I grabbed my purchase and nearly ran to the only open register, paranoid it was going to shut down seconds before I entered the line. I was the final customer to be rung up.

The cashier's name was Dahlila. I had seen her many times over the past two years, but if she recognized me she didn't make note of it.

"We had this come in today," she said, tilting the Polaroid camera in her hands. She made a spectacle of looking through the dirty lens, like a submarine captain gazing through a periscope. "It's marked as antique, so it's going to cost a little extra."

"It's marked as ten dollars," I said. It couldn't have been worth much more.

"Prices change daily. I could ask the manager, but he might have already left for the day. It's going to be at least fifteen."

I knew she was probably going to pocket the five dollars for herself. I didn't care. I reached into my trousers pocket to retrieve my wallet, pulled out what was left of Aunt Kaitlyn's belated birthday gift, and passed it over the counter.

"Have a good day, and thanks for saving lives," she said flatly. She shut her drawer for the final time that day. I failed to notice if she inserted the five dollar bill.

A redneck in a black pickup truck gave me a lift off the side of the road. He seemed disappointed I didn't have any cash to give him, but I wasn't worried. Whether this plan worked or not, this was the last night I was going to spend fretting over Harold and his framed photographs.

Then, a dreaded thought: there would be no film in the camera. How could I have been so careless? And where did you purchase film canisters anyway? It was too late to walk to any major retailers.

I took my chances.

***

It rang and rang and rang. I didn't think it would ever stop. Harry, who must be becoming more frustrated than I was, eventually quit pounding on my bedroom door. I had sought shelter in my room, the camera in my lap. Every so often I would look through the viewfinder with my left eye, practicing taking the shot. It was the type of Polaroid where the print was deposited from the device. An insta-image before the era of smartphones.

I tried playing music on my laptop, but the dominance of the rotary-dial always seemed to override the lyrics no matter how elevated the songs became. Eventually, after my headache subsided, the ringing faded away. I turned off my computer and heard snoring across the hall.

We never kept our bedroom doors locked. There was no need. Aside from sneaking into Harold's room to look at photographs, we never intruded upon one another. Yet still I was shivering as I opened my door, wondering what would happen if he had become suspicious.

Much to my relief it was unlocked. I shoved it open with trembling fingers, camera cradled on one side.

Harold rolled over. His snores were like a baby pig suckling milk from its mother. I didn't know what would happen to him, and I didn't really care. I don't think that made me a horrible person. His life was grand, but mine had become unmanageable.

I raised the camera to my eye socket, focused in on my nemesis, and pressed down. There was a flash that encompassed the darkest parts of the room, then a printing sound. A print exited the camera's mouth and fell to the floor. I looked down; it was milky white, but already the image of a sleeping Harold was bleeding through.

"Patrick, what are you doing?"

He was awake.

I made my escape.

I don't think he ever knew what happened. That was the last time I saw him. I locked my bedroom door and opened the top drawer of my three piece dresser. It was filled with school supplies. I selected a thumb tack and pinned the picture to my wall. It looked ludicrous next to my horror movie posters but hopefully it would serve its purpose.

I slept peacefully.

***

The ringing pierced my eardrums like a hangover after a late night at one of Valdosta's dive bars.

DDDrrrrriiiiinggg!

Normally I would've stuffed my head under my pillow, but that morning was different. I fled my bed with an excitement I have hardly felt before or since. The phone was vibrating with its eagerness to be answered.

"Hello, it's Patrick."

"Patrick, thank God." A chuckle, as if he had forgotten he believed in no such savior. "Can you open the front door? I'm locked outside."

"I'm sorry, my friend. I can't do that."

"But, Patrick, I want to come inside the apartment and I seem to have misplaced my key. Won't you open the door for me?"

"I can't. I won't. You have to stay outside. Now go find your family out there. I don't want to be part of it anymore."

I crushed the receiver into its cradle, unplugged it from the wall, and threw it in the kitchen trash. Still not satisfied, I lifted the trash bag from its container, tied it into a knot, and threw it into Harry's old room without even glancing inside. It could be taken to the dumpster later. For now I was staying indoors.

I didn't go outside the apartment for three days. I was terrified he was waiting for me. I drank away the entire weekend until I was brave enough to wander

46

past the front door.

I never saw or heard from him again.

I passed all my exams and graduated nine months later with a Bachelor of Arts. I began teaching high school the next year, got married to a woman from Illinois, and we have had two children together. I have thought of Harry often but have never spoken of him to my family, even on nights when my wife and I have indulged in more than one bottle of wine.

And I never will.

***

One must be frugal on an educator's salary, so my wife frequents the local thrift markets on weekends and summer afternoons. I always stay home. I either watch the Braves or, on days when she's more persistent, I fake sick. I'm too scared I'll see a green rotary-dial phone. I'm terrified it'll ring and she'll pick it up.

Was I too hard on my friend? I think he was too hard on me. I have a family, and a life outside my old apartment.

And I'm never going to research my real genealogy. I'm horrified if I look too far, he'll be there waiting for me.

"The Portal" by Shikhar Dixit

Me and My Ghost
Fariel Shafee

Steely faced, cruel --she looks at me with
My own eyes, whispers with the lips I know
Are mine too. But only I can see her – a shadow, an
    apparition – that is
There, constantly, like a mocking image of my
    existence. I see a pair of bruised
Hands popping out of her robe, and I know, there is
    something other than
Me in that spirit that's buried beneath those layers.
It wants to kill me, to drag me to a dark land far
    away, and to
Take my place here, in this very world, and I try to
    scream, but I
Don't.
This narrow path is made for me, and so only I can
    see it. No one else can walk
For me
In those worn-out shoes
That day when my ghost and I
Shall have our final fight.

On a Quiet Street, In a Friendly Neighborhood
Jean Jentilet

1:43 a.m.
Motion detected.

Izzy taps the thumbnail image on her phone's screen. The doorbell's view of their front step, driveway, and the bit of street and sidewalk running past their lawn expands. Fifteen seconds of video, not a single movement. She resets the clip, watches again, watches the corners of the viewing area, the sides. Not a single fly. Not one speck of dust. She closes the clip. The stupid thing is too sensitive. Noah set it that way. Once people know it's there, they know to stay out of its field, he said. Setting the sensitivity higher means a better chance of catching someone before they wise up, he said.

Izzy is sure it doesn't work quite like that, but she said nothing at the time because she didn't want the fight. She just wanted the stupid doorbell installed. Every day brings a new complaint on the neighborhood message board about open fence gates, trampled garden beds, and in one particularly upsetting instance, a garage door trundling up and down until the homeowners disabled the door opener altogether. They park in their driveway now. Things are tough all over.

So the doorbell was her idea, but the quantum sensitivity was all Noah. And yet, here she is—*it's the witching hour somewhere*—fielding every alert in the depth of the night, while Noah snores next to her, oblivious. It is very much a metaphor for their marriage. She thinks on it while she tries to fall back asleep. She'll share the revelation with Marissa, their couples counselor. It will annoy Noah. That's fine.

***

Noah appears in the kitchen with sleep-wild hair. He shuffles towards the coffee and lets out a quiet grunt in her direction.

"The doorbell was tilting at windmills again," she says. "Will you please just check the settings again? My phone's lighting up all night."

He raises his steaming mug to his lips and lets out a long sigh. "Sure it didn't pick something up?"

"You can look for yourself when you get around to it, I guess. Just curious, do you want me to wake you up if there's an actual intruder, or just show you the video the next morning?"

"I forgot to turn my alerts back on. It wasn't on purpose." He slurps his coffee. It maddens her. He knows that. "I'll get to it. Are you pissed at me or something?"

You have no idea.

"Just tired." She gathers bags for work up onto her shoulder. "Please fix it, okay? I need some sleep."

"I will. I will." He goes in for a kiss but she turns and he misses. "Love you," he says. "Have a good day, okay?"

"I'll sure try."

***

Another night, another seventeen baseless alerts.

Another morning, another sleep-slow Noah wandering into the kitchen.

"Did you get around to the settings?" Izzy asks. She keeps her voice even and pleasant. It's almost too much.

"I did. And look." Noah slides his phone across the table. "I reset the zones. So it won't go off if the cat lady checks her mail."

"She's our age and she has one cat. And whatever you did, it didn't work. It went off last night more than ever."

"I didn't mean anything by it." He takes his phone

back. "I'll play with the settings some more. Okay? I'm sorry."

"I guess you forgot your alerts again?'

He stares at his phone, machine-gun taps its screen, but does not answer her question.

"Fine," she says.

She leaves without finishing her coffee. At the end of the driveway, she spares a moment to examine the layout of the cat lady's lot. If the cat goes out at night, it can pace around on its own lawn, maybe trigger the doorbell if its tail flicks in the right place. She will ask the cat lady—Anna, she remembers—the next time she sees her.

*****

Izzy pulls into the driveway and notices before anything else a familiar shape squatting on the doorstep, just wide and high enough to block anyone trying to get to the front door. It gives her a moment of pause but not concern. Noah emerges from the garage, smiling. She climbs out of the car and nods towards the front door as he approaches.

"What's going on?" she asks.

"You know that weird plaster guard dog thing we put out for Halloween?"

"Cerberus?"

Noah shakes his head. He is still wrapped up in pride at whatever it is he has done. "Hmm?"

"Cerberus. The three-headed hellhound that we put out for Halloween. It's June. Why's he on our front step? Why's he facing the house?"

"Well..." Noah's chest puffs out just a little. Just enough that the woman who has slept next to him every night for ten years notices it. Just that much, and no more. "I figured it's an easy way to rule out one possibility. If someone's testing the door or playing ding dong ditch or whatever, and beating the camera, then our boy Cerrano—"

"Cerberus."

"Our good boy there stops them. Coming or going they'll have to navigate around him and there's no way to beat the camera then. And even if they try and realize they're busted, we'll get something. We *will* get something. And if we don't, then—"

"Then we do something else. Quickly. Before actual Halloween."

The neighborhood goes wild during the dregs of October. If ever the camera will earn its keep, it will be then.

"Yes. Exactly. Come here." Noah reaches out to her, his beaming smile tugging at something inside her, something in her chest, until she smiles, too. "I turned my alerts on, by the way. And I made veggie burgs. You hungry?"

"Starving," she says.

They walk into the garage, arms wrapped around each other's waists.

***

Izzy sleeps through the night from pure exhaustion. She wakes up in a sun-bright room to an empty bed and a phone screen full of alerts. She finds Noah on the front doorstep, doorbell dangling like an eyeball by the optic nerve of its jumbled wiring.

"What are you doing?"

"What does it look like?" He peers into the shallow socket in the doorframe.

Izzy bites down on the first thing she wants to say.

Looks like someone pretending to know what they're doing.

From Anna's house comes the sound of a garage door rumbling in its tracks. Izzy slips on a pair of sandals from the hodgepodge of footwear near the door. She jogs across the street. As she reaches the other side, Anna steps from the sheltering dimness of her garage.

"Hey, morning."

Anna smiles. "Morning."

"I have a quick question. It's a little strange but it's an issue." Izzy sways as she speaks. *An issue. Yes. It certainly is an issue.* "Our doorbell's been going crazy at night with these alerts, but we don't see anything on the videos. And I thought of your little cat? I thought maybe if the angle's right that she can set it off but we can't see her?"

"Oh no." Anna's neighborly smile inverts and she shakes her head. "Ripley doesn't go out at night. Ever. I've heard of that type of thing, though. Maybe it's a manufacturing defect."

"Maybe." Izzy looks back towards her own house, to Noah crouching and cursing on the doorstep. "Well, if you do catch Ripley sneaking out past her bedtime..."

"Of course."

Izzy crosses back to her side of the street. She is careful to step only in the center of the big pavers that lead from the sidewalk to the front door. The cracks are where the snakes hide, a lesson she learned barefooted during their first spring here.

"Where'd you go?" Noah asks.

"Just across the street. She says her cat never goes out at night."

Noah tilts his head up and looks at her, squinting against the morning sun.

"Did you get the alerts last night?"

"Yeah. I mean..." Izzy slides her phone out of her pocket.

"Did you look at them?"

"I figured there wasn't anything there. As usual."

Noah's face gives away nothing. "Look. Starting at two forty-four."

"Why can't you just tell me what it is?" Izzy does

not try to hide her annoyance as she swipes her phone into life and scrolls. It's too early in the morning to care about smoothing things over.

"Just look. Tell me what you see. Tell me what you see without knowing what to look for." Noah's Adam's apple bobs and his eyes run back and forth between her face and her phone.

2:44 a.m.
Motion detected.
There is nothing in the thumbnail at first glance but there almost never is, even when the thing works. She taps the image but it's the same static view as always. No cats, no people, no actual motion. She moves into the shade of the front step. Maybe she missed something in the glare. She taps the image again.

There is no motion but there is the shape of Cerberus, keeping his off-season guard. The thought crosses her mind that maybe Cerberus moves. Somewhere in all of this, there is a joke at Noah's expense, but she can't find it because she now understands. The shape of Cerberus. Just the shape. The camera's view is unfocused. The entire world is an implication.

"There's a mechanism or something we can adjust? The contrast or something?"

"Three thirteen," Noah says. "The next one."

She swipes her screen. The focus is back in this one, so sharp that Izzy sees the small punctures running up and down the side of the house, marking the path that the supporting screws for Christmas lights take every year and will always take as long as there are Christmases to decorate for and Christmas lights to hang. She sees the dented corner of the mailbox where Noah side-swiped it during his first adventure with a riding mower. The mailbox needs to be replaced but they never get around to it. She sees the sickly green hump at the curb where last weekend's grass clippings have settled into old age waiting for the yard waste truck to make its rounds. She sees what isn't there. She sees why she can see the mailbox and the curb. She looks up from her phone, scans the front step to get her bearings. She wants to blame a lack of coffee, but it's a thin excuse, a weightless thing that offers no comfort.

"Where's Cerberus?" she asks, and she sees the look on Noah's face—the *real* look. Behind the furrowed brow and tight lips that could mean anything, Noah's eyes are windows to a deep confusion being swallowed by something meaner.

"I don't know," he says, "but I know that this fucking thing is going back to the store and whoever took that dog..." He tugs at the junction of two wires twisted together like death-locked fingers. "Post something on the community board. Or don't. I don' know. Whoever's doing this shit'll wish they'd just skipped to the next house. Fuck with me. Assholes."

"As ominous as that sounds, why don't we see if the problem doesn't get solved with a new doorbell." Izzy is grateful for the distraction of keeping him level. It keeps her from looking too closely at the things spinning up in her own head. "That way we can post actual pictures instead of weird insinuations."

"Fine." He yanks the death-locked wires apart. "Can you at least find the receipt?"

He does not look up as she steps over his legs and through the front door. He's angry because she's made a point.

Marissa has her work cut out for her.

***

They eat dinner in silence. The nicks and scratches on his hands testify to his impatience. The

56

doorbell sits between them in its box, repacked to retail-ready perfection.

After dinner, they watch television. They go through their nightly routines without any words passing between them but an occasional "Excuse me" or the odd "Sorry, I need to reach here."

In the spare bedroom that she uses as an office, Izzy goes through the short cabinet that holds the few undigitized things in her life—birth certificates, marriage license, passports, the receipt for the doorbell. She tucks the receipt into the doorbell's box so that it sticks up like a child's raised hand in the front row of a bashful classroom. She leaves the box on the kitchen table. She knows he'll ask her where it is in the morning anyway. She'll mention this to Marissa, too. The list grows.

Izzy slips into bed next to Noah's fuming back. Her mind loses its hold on the waking world, and from the gravity well of sleep, it whispers to her, and asks her how many more nights like this she thinks there will be.

***

The mattress sighs and relaxes as he slides off. Izzy knows without opening her eyes that he is in front of the dresser by the light creak of a floorboard. She senses the door opening, the sudden feeling of the empty space of the hallway looming a yard from her feet. She hears the quiet click of the door closing again, and knows she is alone. She opens her eyes. Dark, but for the few stray bits of streetlight sneaking past blinds. She checks her phone.

2:02.

Her heart lifts with delight. No alerts. She remembers that the thing sits blind and deaf and mute in its box on the kitchen table. She lays in the stillness of the empty bed for as long as she can stand it. Sleep does not return, so she rises and moves across the room, using much more care than Noah, and misses all the weak spots in the floor. She is little more than a shadow drifting through the house and down the stairs. She stops just short of stepping off the stairs and into the living room.

Noah sits on a chair he has taken from the kitchen and placed next to the front door, with the chair's back against the wall under a sidelight. He is leaning forward, his face pressing against the sidelight curtain, and Izzy can tell by the angle of his head that he is peering through the sliver of space between the curtain and the side of the window. She begins to speak, hitches the air into her lungs and forms the intention in her throat.

What are you doing?

She holds it back. This is not a fight for the small hours of the morning. She turns and creeps back up the stairs, eyes on Noah for as long as he is within her field of view. He does not move.

***

Izzy and Noah move around each other in the kitchen like strangers in a shop, getting their coffee and protein bars, checking their phones, finding things to look at besides each other.

"I put the receipt in the box," Izzy says. The awkwardness of the situation transcends her irritation. She cannot leave for her day without *something.*

"I saw." Noah speaks into his mug, but at least he speaks. "Have you looked out front?"

"Why?"

For the first time in a day, their eyes meet. He glances towards the front door. She follows his look with her eyes and sees their foyer exactly as she had left it early that morning, *sans* the night-stalking husband perched at the front door. He nods. She

58

sighs and starts across the foyer. Two steps from the door, she knows why he wants her to look for herself. She pushes back a sidelight curtain and sees that she's right. Cerberus sits with his face towards the door and his back to the street, exactly as Noah had placed him the other day. Izzy takes a sip of a coffee and a deep breath and squares her shoulders before turning to face her husband again.

"They brought him back," she says. This is the simple truth. The dog was gone, and now the dog is back. There is no need for a nasty post to the community board. There is no need for anything but a new doorbell. There is certainly no need for the half-formed thought twitching in the back of her mind.

Noah blinks at her over the top of his phone.

"No one brought him back," he says. "He just...was there."

Izzy shrugs. She goes to the sink and rinses out her mug. "The doorbell was gone. Whoever took the dog saw a chance to put it back without drama. So, they did. Problem solved. Moving on."

"Sure. Yeah. Sure." Noah stands. He looks into his mug. "The doorbell was gone. The doorbell was in the box. Sending me alerts."

The thing at the back of her mind runs forward and takes a breath and spews forth everything it can manage—*This is a game a stupid game it's all a stupid game I hate you please just put the old doorbell back because I'm sick of this and I'm sick of you and I just want to go to work*—before fading back behind reassurances.

Mountains from molehills. Always making mountains from molehills, Noah. Always.

"That's impossible. Look, I have to go. I'm already late. Can we deal with this later?"

He is next to her before she realizes he has even

stood. He pushes his phone towards her face. "Impossible." A list of alerts roll into the endlessness beyond the bounds of the screen. He swipes and swipes and swipes and they keep coming.

"I didn't get any." She can think of nothing else to say.

"When was the last time you updated the app?"

"I—"

She cannot remember. She remembers installing it and maybe she updated it without thinking about it but she cannot say for sure. Noah doesn't wait for her to figure it out.

"I ignored them at first," he says. "I figured it was something in the app. Had to be something in the app. No other explanation." Noah pockets his phone and leans against the sink so that he faces her as he speaks. "But by then I'm awake. So I come down here. I don't know why. Don't know what I was thinking. Maybe I'd get a beer. Just a nudge in the right direction. Alert goes off as I hit the bottom of the stairs so I go to the door. Nothing. I go into the app. Live view. Nothing. But it won't stop. Alerts keep coming. And then I feel like I'm being watched."

"Middle of the night. You were half asleep," Izzy says. She will not admit that she was the one doing the watching.

"No. No. Somebody's fucking with us. Somebody's hacked into our wifi or something. I sat there all night, looking out that window." Noah points towards the door. "All night, alerts. All night, nothing. And then, I blinked. And the dog was there."

"You blinked?" Izzy asks. "You sure you didn't nod off?"

Noah's shoulders and chest rise with a deep breath that he blows out like a kiss.

"I'm sure."

He pushes off the counter and snatches the box

from the kitchen table. "I'm taking care of this once and for all."

He slams the door connecting the garage and the kitchen. His car's engine starts and fades down the street. Izzy looks at her own phone.

One alert. Just one. The thumbnail is a black square. She taps it.

Connection lost.

It's nothing.

***

Izzy stays at the office later than she needs to. There, she can be alone with her thoughts. In her cubicle, with all of her colleagues already sitting down at their own dinner tables, she can enjoy this time where other people's existences do not bump against hers, do not crowd her peace, her *being*, with their own desperate needs for affirmation, for acknowledgment. She can listen to nothing. She can see only what she wants to see.

Her phone buzzes.

No. No.

She refuses to look at it. There is nothing anyone can want from her now that cannot wait. All of it can wait.

Her phones falls silent again but the moment is gone. Her peace is gone. She picks up the phone.

6:34 p.m.
Motion detected.

She taps the thumbnail. Movement hints from the bottom edge of the doorbell's vision. Their street is dark, another time zone from the still-light summer evening cooling outside the wide windows that she can see when she peeks out of her cube. Noah's face appears. He smiles. He waves. He points at the street behind him and ducks back down. The clip stops and slides back to the beginning.

She taps a message into her phone.

I saw you. I'll be home soon.

Noah answers with a smiley, the one she always thinks of as the shit-eating emoji.

In her car, she gives herself a few more sweet moments of nothing before she starts the engine and steers towards home.

***

Cerberus still sits with his back to the street. Izzy squeezes past him. A tiny blue dot lights up above the new doorbell to acknowledge her presence. Her phone buzzes from her purse a split second later.

"So far, so good," Noah says from the doorway. "It's the next model up, by the way. Guy at the store said there were a lot of complaints about the old model."

"What about the app?" Izzy asks.

"Updated that again, too. So should you."

Izzy steps through the doorway. The good smells of dinner greet her.

"Maybe we'll get some real sleep tonight," she says.

Noah grunts and locks the door behind her.

"Maybe," he says.

***

"Goddamnit! I am done. Done!"

A riot of sheets and cursing yank Izzy from a blank, silent sleep, and now she is awake, and the chaos next to her assures no return to her previous state.

"What's going on?" She is off guard. She does not have the resources to process what is happening.

Noah jumps up from the bed. "You're not getting them?" He paces to the dresser and pulls something out of the top drawer. "The alerts? Four hundred and thirty-two. Four hundred and thirty-two! It hasn't stopped! Haven't you heard?"

62

She cannot form an answer. He is out the door now, now he pounds down the stairs.

She pushes off the covers and snatches her phone from the nightstand. She doesn't look at it, but follows Noah's clamor downstairs. She steps onto the first landing. The metallic click of the lock releasing on the front door echoes up to her. She turns the corner and takes the remaining steps two at a time.

The foyer floor is cold, too cold. Not air-conditioning cold, but winter cold, brittle and bone-deep. Noah throws the front door open. Izzy braces for a gust of chill wind. Thick summer night oozes in instead. The empty front step is as still as a painting.

"I'm done playing around." Izzy only recognizes the growl as Noah's because it takes the shape of words. "You'll wish I'd called the fucking cops."

Noah steps through the door and sinks into the night.

He does not charge down the driveway or sprint across the lawn. He is simply not there.

Izzy blinks.

He is gone.

Swallowed whole.

She steps across the frigid tiles. Her numbing toes stub against the high threshold. She stops.

"Noah."

Her voice falls into dead air between the foyer and the front step. She lifts a foot. Her phone buzzes. She steps backwards, away from the door. She brings the phone close to her face and swipes it open.

2:39 a.m.
Motion detected.

She turns off her phone and peers into the night. There is nothing. As usual.

She shuts the door.

You don't have to be a house to be haunted.
— Emily Dickinson, 1830-1886, American poet

Winter Traveller
Sarah Cannavo

She offered to lead me
through the storm to shelter
and gratefully I followed,
until glancing down I saw
only my tracks in the snow.

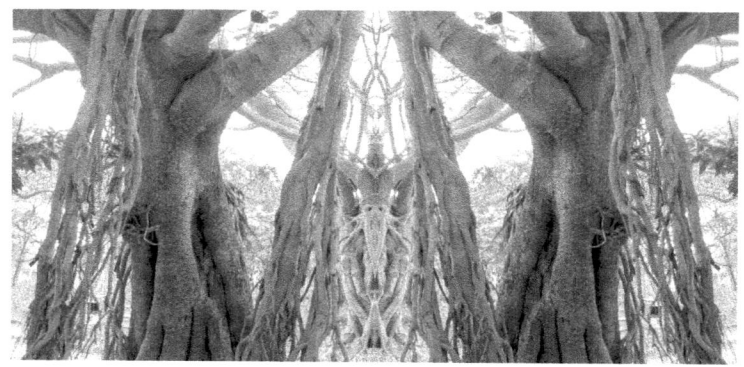

"The Great Charmer" by Sonali Roy

Protective Shadow
DJ Tyrer

"So, you're moving in?" The voice had come from behind the unruly hedge that ran beside the path to the front door of the house and Sam found himself staring, attempting to make out who'd spoken.

A head, that of an older man, maybe about sixty, with salt-and-pepper hair and a moustache that bristled like the hedge, popped up. Sam guessed the man must be standing on tiptoe.

"Hello, I'm Keith. I must be your neighbour."

There was a rustle and a hand, clad in a thick gardening glove, thrust itself through the hedge. Sam shook it.

"Hi. I'm Sam. Yeah, I'm moving in, today."

"Excellent. Excellent. It'll be good to have someone in there after so long. Empty houses always seem to attract the vandals and glue-sniffers, and we don't want any of them about, do we? No, it'll be good to see it occupied."

"Yes, well, it's going to take a little effort; it's been allowed to get into a state."

"A real shame. I don't know why it stood empty so long. It's a historical treasure."

"Yes, it does look quite old."

"It is. Parts of it are seventeenth century, you know."

"I didn't. Really?"

"Yes. Of course, it's been added to – Victorian and Edwardian, and more recently – but, there's still a little of the original in there. A little slice of history. Did they tell you?"

"What?"

"We call it the witch house."

"The witch house?"

"Yes. Back when it was built, when this was a village, not part of London, a witch lived there. Well, they called her a witch, but you know what people were like back then, superstitious lot. Claimed she kept a demon as a pet. She probably just had a black cat and annoyed the wrong person. They hanged her."

"Poor woman."

"Indeed. Still, it makes for a good story, something to tell guests."

"I guess so. Oh, well, I must be getting on."

"Welcome to the neighbourhood."

"Thanks."

Chuckling, Sam went inside. A little paint and the house would be tolerable. There was a smell of damp that he would have to investigate, but the place was sound enough.

There was a sound from the back of the house and Sam jumped.

"Stupid." The talk of witches had made him nervous. Childish.

He headed into the kitchen and stopped in surprise.

"How did you get in here?" he asked the sleek black cat that was stretching out in a patch of sunlight.

"Do you come with the house? Well, you can't belong to the people who used to live here. Are you a witch's cat? You're the right colour."

It had rolled itself onto its feet and was weaving around his legs, rubbing its cheek against him. He crouched down and fondled its head. It purred and pushed back against him.

"Well, I guess you and I can be friends. I'll ask Keith if he knows who you belong to."

Keith didn't and there was no response to the posters he put up around the neighbourhood. The

66

cat, Sam had jokingly taken to calling it Ginger in a fit of contrariness, occasionally stepped out into the jungle-thick garden, but never ventured further away and very clearly had chosen the house to be its new home, too. Sam wasn't going to argue.

But, as pleasant as the house was once he'd made progress with the decorating, and as much as he enjoyed the company of Ginger, Sam wasn't entirely happy. It wasn't just the long hours of data entry and the awful commute, although he often felt as if his arms would drop off by the time he got home and his temper was badly frayed. Indeed, the welcome the sleek black feline provided him with every day helped to heal the latter. There was the damp, which was proving stubbornly resistant to treatment and formed a black stain of mould in the corner of the dining room, like some shadowy beast crouching waiting to pounce. And, there were the noises: at first, he'd thought it might be the vandals Keith had spoken of, but he'd searched the house and garden more than once and come to the conclusion it was the scratching of mice; he hoped Ginger might deal with them. But, more than those, there was the way he never felt quite right and his sleep always seemed disturbed, and not just by the mice, although, in neither case, could he quite describe what was wrong. He wondered if maybe he was coming down with something.

"If it wasn't for you, Ginge," Sam said, yawning, as he stroked the cat that lay sprawled upon his lap, "I think my blood pressure would make my head explode."

Suddenly, Ginger shifted its weight and changed its position so that it was looking up at him. Ginger did that, sometimes, for no clear reason. The cat was tense, solid muscle beneath the sleek black fur, as if it were ready to leap at something. Then, a thought struck Sam: the cat wasn't looking at him, but past him, over his shoulder.

Sam turned his head and looked. He'd half-expected to see someone there, behind him, in the doorway, but it was empty. He felt foolish, but a little nervous, too.

"I guess you're seeing things, eh, Ginge?" He reached out to caress the cat's head, but it hissed. "Oh, sorry."

Now he considered it, he guessed Ginger had always been looking behind him, through the doorway to the dining room. The damp: it must catch a whiff; it wasn't pleasant.

"Mystery solved," he chuckled.

The cat hissed as if to deny it.

"Okay, have it your way."

Eventually, the cat settled down, it always did. Sam resolved to tackle the damp just as soon as he'd the time. Not that it seemed he'd have any anytime soon; he hadn't even found time to burn the loose wood and other detritus from the house as a bonfire, yet.

But, while he hadn't the time for that task, Sam had decided to tackle the problem of his disturbed sleep. He'd read about 'mindfulness' in the 'paper and had decided to give it a go, trying to clear and calm his mind each night before he went to sleep.

It didn't seem to be working. In fact, things seemed to be getting worse and he seemed to find himself slipping down into dark and formless dreams that left a sense of unpleasantness and uncleanness in their wake despite a lack of any discernable elements to them beyond their darkness. It was a little like being in a dank, unlit pit where you could see nothing, but just knew you were surrounded by muck and filth. It was probably the stress, but Sam wondered if the smell of the damp, or perhaps the inhalation of mould spores, were also to blame.

Sam found himself sinking, once more, down in the black morass of unpleasantness; only, this time, it seemed to have gained form. He seemed to be in a room similar to his lounge, although it was shadowy and uncertain, as if he were looking at it through sleep-rimed eyes. He was fairly sure he was dreaming. The horrible sensation still haunted him. It felt almost as if he were being watched: Watched by some invisible and malevolent presence...

He shivered. Did you shiver in dreams?

Sam looked around, but couldn't see anything awful in the room. That didn't help and he shivered again. Somehow, the absence of something malevolent only made the feeling worse.

Sam stumbled through the doorway into the dining room. Still nothing. Not that he could see the room clearly, it was so murky.

"I'd really like to wake up now," he muttered.

As if in answer to his plea, he heard a manic chuckle.

"Who's there?" He glanced wildly about, but still couldn't see who or what tormented him. The chuckling seemed to echo all around him and there was a scratching sound, too, as if something were clawing at the walls, trying to get out. Or, in.

Suddenly, something brushed against his leg. Sam shrieked and jerked his leg away in surprise.

Then, he realised it was a sleek, black shape that was moving about his feet.

"Ginger? Is that you?"

There was an answering meow and he felt a surge of reassurance, the cloying sensation that had grasped him seeming to shrink back. The chuckling stopped.

The cat yowled and tugged at his pyjama leg.

"Okay. Okay. Lead and I'll follow."

The cat seemed almost to skim along the floor like a lithe shadow and Sam stumbled after it, not knowing where it led, but not wanting to be left behind.

They seemed to be twisting their way through strangely-curved corridors that were like some gothic maze. Sam soon lost all sense of direction. He felt so disorientated, he was almost uncertain which way was up and, at times, it seemed almost as if he were floating along, dragged forwards by the cat's wake.

Then, he was falling. Or, possibly, rising. Moving. He couldn't quite be sure of the direction, or why. He was spinning in shadow.

There was a sudden pain in his hand and his eyes snapped open. Sam closed them again, wincing, dazzled by the bright morning sunlight, then tentatively reopened them. He was lying on his bed. Ginger was lying by his side, head turned to regard him with bright, deep eyes. Sam looked at his hand: a set of parallel scratches marred it, left by Ginger's claw.

"Ouch!" He rubbed vigorously at it, then fumbled himself off the bed and staggered through to the bathroom to wash his hand.

"You'll give me tetanus doing that, you silly cat," he shouted back to Ginger, who was busy stretching out across the duvet. But, despite his annoyance, he couldn't help but think that the cat's claws had saved him from the horrible dream. Or, was he confusing dream-Ginger with the real cat that had scratched it? By the time he headed downstairs for breakfast, he had no idea, having turned dream and reality over so many times in his mind that he was quite confused.

Not that he held onto either the question or the dream as he dashed out of the house to catch his train. His days were too busy to spend them worrying about his nights and he'd quite forgotten about it all by the time he arrived home to eat and drowse in front of the telly and, then, stumble up to bed.

"Night, Ginge." He patted the cat before sinking down into sleep.

But, his dream hadn't forgotten him and Sam found himself, once more, in a shadowy room that might have been his lounge. The details of the room seemed a little clearer, more formed, yet it was just as murky as before. It made Sam think of documentaries featuring sunken wrecks: It was as if he were observing his surroundings through dark and silty water. Not that he felt any water, but did dreams have to make sense? Perhaps he was wandering through his house after some immense, Biblical flood? That was as logical as anything that happened in a dream.

Perhaps, he reflected, if that were the nature of his dream, then it explained the peculiar, horrible sensation that accompanied it. It was the sort of feeling he imagined would accompany being stalked by a shark. But, still there was no sign of the source of the malevolence, nor, murkiness aside, anything else to support his aquatic conjectures.

For reasons he couldn't quite understand, and in spite of the way he otherwise seemed detached from his dream state, Sam found himself stumbling into the dining room. It was as if some force were dragging him along.

The sense that something evil was watching him was stronger here, but he still couldn't see what. Then, he turned towards the corner with the damp stain and saw... something, a dark shadow hidden within the murk, crouching there.

Sam recoiled and nearly fell as something, a second something, seemed to coil itself about his legs.

He looked down and saw a serpentine blackness

71

that was, he realised, the cat.

"Ginger?" he managed to gasp.

A yowl answered him and the cat streaked off. He followed it as quickly as he could. Occasionally, it would pause and look back at him, as if demanding he hurry up. He hurried.

Once again, he was stumbling his way through a peculiar, dark labyrinth of tunnels that twisted and turned in a maddening manner until he felt as if his head were spinning and he no longer knew which way was up and he was floating, spinning, rising and falling...

Then, a pain. He gasped and opened his eyes and clutched his hand. He was in his bedroom, in the dark, and his hand was damp with blood. He heard Ginger hiss. He sat up, confused.

There was something crouched at the foot of his bed. Not Ginger; he could see the dark arch of the hissing cat beside him, but something else, ape-like, perhaps, he couldn't tell. Was he back in his dream?

Then, it was gone and he was blinking sleep from his eyes, uncertain how long he'd been awake. Ginger was coiling about his legs, proprietarily. Then, the cat yowled and tugged at his pyjama leg, just as it had in his dream.

"What is it?" Sam mumbled.

Ginger yowled back, as if annoyed, tugged again, then leapt down from the bed.

Sam made a decision and tumbled off the bed in pursuit of the cat, which slid out of the bedroom and, then, down the stairs like a shadow. He ran after it, following it into the lounge and, then, the dining room.

Ginger ran towards the corner with the damp and hissed. In the faint light of the pre-dawn, the pattern of mould looked like more than just a stain. Sam shuddered: The shape was horribly like that he'd seen, or dreamt he'd seen, at the foot of his bed. The cat was hissing at it as if it were more than just a damp patch.

"What is it?" He wished Ginger could speak, explain. Maybe he would, if this was all still part if his dream. He was so confused.

The cat turned its head back to look at him, as if willing him to understand, then turned back to face the wall, hissed one more time, then threw itself at the wall, scratching and spitting.

Maybe this was real. Maybe this was a dream. Either way, Sam reached another decision: Ginger seemed to have a motivation, even if he'd no idea what it was, and he'd heed it.

Sam looked about. There was a standard lamp in the corner of the room. He seized it and wielded it like a sledgehammer, smashing the base into the damp plaster, rapidly breaking a hole in the wall. The plaster appeared to have straw or hair in it and had been smeared across a wickerwork-like wooden frame: The wall, he realised, must date to the earliest stages of the house.

Wood shattered and a void was revealed. And, within the space, something sat. A something that had a horribly familiar shape to it. Sam wasn't sure what he was looking at – something large and ape-like – but, he was certain he'd seen it, or its shadow, before.

A wave of nausea surged through him and Sam let the standard lamp slip from his fingers to clatter to the floor at his feet. Ginger jumped back at the sound, then returned to coil protectively about his legs. Sam stared at the thing in the hole, trying to process it.

For a moment, he imagined it must be the body of the witch, but he knew that was unlikely and it didn't look like the mummified corpse of an old woman. It was squat and heavily-built, like an ape, and had clearly been sealed in the wall for ages; it seemed completely desiccated. It was difficult to make out details in the darkness of the recess, but he thought it seemed rodent-like and there seemed to be parchment-like membranes attached to the arms. A bat? It looked too large and heavy, but...

Ginger hissed. The thing seemed to twitch.

There was a sound that mixed the ripping of paper with the creak of an unoiled hinge as the mummified thing raised its head and looked at him with eyes that appeared to be no more than black, ragged holes in its long-dead face.

Sam screamed. It lunged towards him. Ginger leapt.

For a moment, Sam felt as if he'd been enveloped inside a vast paper bag, pressing in on him, suffocating him, while a dry, dusty breath rattled into his face. He tried to scream again, but his lungs were being crushed. Although it seemed fragile, he couldn't seem to fight free of it or tear through the wing-like membranes.

Then, he was free and the thing was tumbling away from him, the black shadow of a cat writhing atop the grey, leathery shape.

For a moment, Sam was too stunned to react. Then, he grabbed the standard lamp, again, and swung it, smashing it against the thing that struggled beneath the cat. He managed to stumble upright and over to it. The thing, suddenly, seemed far less scary, flapping weakly beneath the manically-hissing and clawing cat.

Sam raised the lamp and slammed its base straight down into the thing's head. It shuddered. He slammed the lamp down again and it fell still. The cat slipped off of it and Sam kept bludgeoning it until the head was a ragged mess that didn't look much

74

different to the fragmented plaster of the wall.

He set down the standard lamp and leant against it, breathing heavily, watching carefully for any sign of movement. It was still.

Sam still couldn't decide what it was. His best guess was some kind of bizarre, mutant bat. Had it been alive all this time, in some sort of hibernation, or...? He didn't dare consider it further. A connection to the witch seemed obvious, yet also madness. But, then, the entire night's events had been madness, and he still wasn't certain what had been real and what dream.

He was, at least, certain it was dead.

Not that Sam was going to take any chances. He decided to burn it: There was a pile of old wood, cabinet doors and other rubbish from the house that he'd been meaning to make a bonfire of. He didn't care if Keith objected.

"Watch it," he told Ginger. The cat seemed to nod in understanding.

It didn't take long to build the bonfire and get it alight. Sam used a spade to lift the battered, desiccated remains of the bat-thing into a wheelbarrow and wheeled it over to the fire, tipping it onto it, before dosing it with accelerant.

He watched it burn with a grin smile of satisfaction as the flames sent shadows dancing about the garden and the sleek black shape of the cat danced among them.

As the fire died down to smouldering ashes and the sun illuminated the scene, banishing the horrors of the night, Ginger returned to its position at his feet, coiling about them, purring as it rubbed against him.

Sam crouched down and gave the cat a grateful and vigorous stroke.

"Thanks, Ginge; I think you saved my life."

The cat yowled up at him, as if to say he was welcome.

That was the last Sam saw of Ginger. The cat didn't follow him back into the house and wasn't in the garden when he went to look for it. It was as if, job done, it had gone, melting away with the night before the blazing dawn sun.

Perhaps, he thought, later, it was for the best. Sam repaired the wall and was able to pretend nothing had ever happened, get on with his life. But, regardless, he missed the cat, and, though he owned many more, none ever quite filled the hole it left in his heart. But, every now and then, Sam would see a sleek, serpentine shadow and, though, when he looked closer, it was never more than a trick of the light, he liked to think Ginger was still around, watching over him, his own personal, protective shadow.

"Nature's Rooftop" by Sonali Roy

Hot Dog and Ectoplasm
Alicia Hilton

My dog and I share an addiction—ectoplasm.
There's no greater joy for a corgi with a sixth sense
than hunting ghosts in Central Park.
Luna yipped at auras while ordinary dogs chased
    balls.

A snort of spiritual essence from an apparition
    wearing a pinstripe suit
strolling past the zoo. A dead ringer for Frank
    Sinatra.
I opened my jaws wide and inhaled shimmering
    euphoria.
Ol' Blue Eyes tasted like starlight and lemon
    meringue pie.

The sun was setting when Luna and I arrived at the
    pond.
No other pedestrians saw the phantom grab the
    woman feeding the ducks.
The ghost's gray aura turned crimson when corgi
    jaws chomped his leg.
Some spirits bleed. Tail-wagging deliciousness.

The Ghost on Coffin Street
Roxanne Dent

It was the beginning of August when the Miller's moved into their two hundred-year old, Victorian home on Coffin Street in Haverhill, Massachusetts. The house backed on Woods and an ancient graveyard.

On moving day there was a terrible storm. The wind howled down the block and snaked its way into the cracks of the old house whining and screaming like a lost child. The beautiful, old, oak tree broke in half when lightning struck. The electricity went out.

Superstitious people might take it as a bad sign. But the Miller's didn't have a superstitious bone in their collective bodies. Trudy was a Physician's Assistant at Massachusetts General Hospital. Her husband Frank worked for a high-tech company as a computer analyst. Trudy worked out at a gym every day and Frank jogged every night in all weather. Cheerful, friendly, and social they were quickly accepted into the community. The only fly in the ointment was their daughter, Zoe.

Moody, demanding and selfish, Zoe called them Trudy and Frank, rather than mom and dad and threw colossal temper tantrums when she didn't get her way.

Unlike her parents, Zoe wasn't into fitness. She never exercised or played sports. Her parents gently urged her to go on a diet, but Zoe refused. When they refused to buy junk food, she wouldn't speak to them for a week. They despaired and often wondered if someone had switched babies on them in the hospital.

The move to Coffin Street took place when Zoe

was twelve. It wasn't long before she heard stories of how her house stood on the market for years because it was haunted.

Like her parents, Zoe wasn't superstitious. She acknowledged slasher movies scared her. But the good ones were supposed to scare you. Believing in ghosts was dumb.

***

On a beautiful, sunny day near the end of summer, Zoe's parents invaded her sanctuary.

"The neighborhood block party starts at four," Trudy reminded her.

"So," Zoe muttered.

"It's the perfect time to make friends before school starts," her mother suggested tentatively.

"I wouldn't need to make friends at all if we hadn't moved. And you barged right into my room without knocking. Just leave me alone," she screamed.

Her parents exchanged looks and walked out, shutting the door behind them.

Zoe threw an empty jar of pistachios at the wall. A piece of the wall popped out. The space wasn't very large, but inside Zoe discovered a heart shaped locket on a gold chain. To Zoe's disappointment, when she pried it open, there was only a single strand of fair hair. She was about to show her prize to her parents but decided it would be her secret. Searching through her photo albums, she found a picture of her and Poppa at Christmas. Her grandfather was the only one who had loved her unconditionally. Thinking about him still brought tears to her eyes. Tossing the blonde hair in the garbage, she cut and placed the picture inside the locket.

***

In September, Zoe attended school. Mr. Leonard, the English teacher made an announcement.

"There's a school-wide writing competition for Halloween which is only a month away. The winner of the best ghost story receives a new laptop donated by Marshall's Electronics."

Zoe decided right away she would win it and impress the class with a really scary story. Since she didn't believe in ghosts, she was going to have to do some research. She felt she had an advantage with a graveyard that was practically in her own back yard. As soon as school let out, Zoe headed straight for the woods to soak up atmosphere and look for inspiration. How hard could it be?

The thick trees abruptly opened out into a clearing. Cracked and crumbling, grey, and black stones stuck half out of the frozen ground. Zoe tried to read the dates, but years of rain and snow wore most of the writing away. Determined to succeed, she sat down on one of the broken stones and leaned against a tree. Removing her favorite gold pen and red, spiral notebook, she waited to be inspired.

The wind gradually let up and the sun was hot on her back. After a while, Zoe's eyes began to close. The pen and book slipped to the ground.

A rustling sound startled her. Zoe sat up rubbing her eyes, realizing she must have dozed. It was starting to get dark. A sudden gust of wind whistled through the shimmering piles of leaves as if keening for the dead.

Zoe shivered and stood up, stamping her feet in the cold. Sitting in a cold graveyard was crazy when she could be in her kitchen eating a warm pop tart before supper. She caught sight of a figure in the shadows and blinked, wondering if she imagined it.

The figure emerged from the woods and stared back at her. It was a girl about her own age with butter blonde curls down past her waist that whipped back and forth in the wind. She wore a long, black, velvet dress with a white, lace collar and boots. The girl seemed to glide towards her and for a split second, Zoe felt a flash of fear. The fear made her angry and she frowned as the girl stood before her.

It didn't help that she was very pretty in a pale way, with cerulean, blue eyes, and thick lashes. Zoe glared at her resentfully. The girl spoke first in an oddly formal voice.

"How do you do. My name is Violet."

"I'm..."

"Zoe," Violet finished. "I know."

Zoe hated to be at a disadvantage. "You're not in my class. I've never seen you before

Violet smiled. She had perfect teeth and a dimple in her right cheek. "I'd like to be your friend."

Zoe was instantly suspicious. "Why?"

"I can help you with your ghost story."

"I don't need any help." The wind picked up and Zoe shivered. Even with her down jacket, she couldn't control the shivers. Violet was only wearing a dress. "Aren't you cold?"

Violet laughed. "Not anymore."

Her laugh was a tinkling sound, reminding Zoe of the time her father knocked icicles off their roof after a blizzard. It was creepy.

"Where do you live?" Zoe asked.

"Here," Violet said.

"No, you don't. This is a cemetery."

"I used to live over there," Violet said pointing toward Zoe's house.

"That's my house."

Violet giggled. "I saw you when you found the locket."

"No you didn't. No one was there."

Violet sighed. "I was standing right beside you."

"I was all alone," Zoe said, pleased she caught the girl in a lie but puzzled how she knew about the locket.

"I thought you would have guessed by now."

"Guessed what?" Zoe said annoyed.

Violet circled Zoe, skipping over the broken stones as she sang,

I do not like to boast but I really am a ghost.

"No you're not. Ghosts aren't real," Zoe said firmly and turned away.

"That's why you can't write a good ghost story," Violet mocked.

When Zoe looked back, Violet was gone. She peered into the gloom, but the girl had vanished. Shaken in spite of her refusal to believe in ghosts, Zoe told herself Violet must be hiding behind one of the marble stones that remained standing.

Either Violet was mental or somebody at school had put her up to playing a joke on the new, fat girl. Zoe quickly walked back to the house. When she got inside, she shut and double locked the door.

Violet's voice echoed down the stairs. "I like what you did with our room."

Zoe jumped. Sheer primitive terror sent her scurrying for cover. She ducked into the mud room and shut and locked the door, cowering behind the skis, coats, and boots, hugging her legs to her. It was Friday and her mother wouldn't be home for hours. She didn't have her cell phone on her, and her mother would laugh if she said she was hiding from a ghost.

Violet's eerie voice sounded right outside the door. "I can prove I'm a ghost. Want to see?"

"Go away," Zoe screamed.

She watched horrified as Violet's legs and arms materialized through the door, followed by her head and the rest of her body, until she stood in front of Zoe. Her eyes glowed in the dark.

Zoe whimpered.

"Don't be afraid." Violet stroked Zoe's hair and watched her tremble. Violet's touch was like a wisp of icy fog. "You can visit me at the cemetery any time." I don't come here very often."

Zoe kept her eyes squeezed tightly shut but Violet didn't speak or touch her again. After a few seconds, she risked opening them. Violet was gone.

Although there was no sign Violet had ever been there, Zoe knew she hadn't imagined it. She desperately wanted a cup of hot chocolate with whipped cream and a couple of mallow mars.

Once she finished the hot chocolate and four mallow mars, Zoe felt a lot calmer. Now that the initial shock wore off, she believed what she'd witnessed was a real ghost. She had a lot of questions she wanted to ask Violet the next time they met.

The following day was Saturday. Zoe leapt out of bed a good two hours before she normally did, excited at the prospect of meeting Violet again and just a little bit nervous. As soon as Zoe reached the graveyard, Violet appeared.

"I'm sorry if I frightened you yesterday," Violet said.

"It was a shock at first," Zoe admitted. She whipped out a chocolate chip muffin and removing the paper, took a bite as she asked her first question. "Are ghosts ever hungry?"

"Not for food."

"For what then?"

"Lost dreams."

"That's stupid. When you die, don't you go to Heaven or something?"

"Not everyone moves on."

"How long have you been a ghost?"

"A hundred and fifty years," Violet said as she perched on top of a broken headstone and swung her legs back and forth.

"That's a long time. You must miss your family."

Violet stopped swinging her legs and jumped down, landing a couple of inches from Zoe, her sapphire eyes dark. "Unlike you, I didn't have a real family. My mother died giving birth to me and my father shot himself six months later."

"That's awful," Zoe said. She stepped back, wishing she hadn't asked.

"Uncle Josiah, my father's brother took me in."

"That was nice." Zoe said.

Violet began twirling a curl around and around her finger. "That big marble stone over thee is his." She turned abruptly and began walking away.

"Wait," Zoe shouted standing up. "Where are you going?" Violet kept walking.

"A day didn't go by Uncle Josiah let me forget I was the cause of my parent's deaths. He beat me with a leather belt and switches whenever he drank. Every night I prayed to God he'd die."

Zoe rushed to keep up. She truly felt sorry for Violet. Pulling the locket out from under her pink camisole, she asked, "Does this belong to you?"

Violet glanced at it. "It was my mother's."

"I suppose you want it back," Zoe said with a sigh and removed it.

Violet's hand reached out, brushing Zoe's neck with icy fingers, making her jump. "No," she screamed. Zoe froze.]

Taking a deep breath, Violet's whole demeanor relaxed. "Finders Keepers," she said with a brilliant smile, her eyes sparkling and dimples in her cheek showing.

Zoe didn't have any previous experience with ghosts, so she wasn't sure what to make of Violet's abrupt change of mood. As Violet handed the locket back, it popped open, and she stared at the picture of

Poppa and Zoe.

"Who is that with you?"

"My grandfather." Zoe thought it very generous of Violet to let her keep an heirloom. "How did you die? I mean if you want to talk about it," she added politely as she closed the locket and replaced it inside her jacket next to her heart.

Violet's pale, dainty fingers plucked at the lace at her throat. "I was twelve like you. It was winter and I developed pneumonia. To make sure I didn't recover, Uncle Josiah dismissed the servants, opened the windows in my room and locked me in. I suffered for days before I died."

"Your uncle murdered you?" Zoe was shocked.

"He did. When I became a ghost, I appeared to him sometimes. His drinking got worse." Violet smiled. The smile gave Zoe the creeps. ""But after he died, I didn't think about him at all." She floated past Zoe to the edge of the clearing where she stared out at the roofs of the houses. "What I missed most in life was a family who loved me. I never stopped wanting that." Turning to face Zoe, she stared at her with a strange look.

"What?" Zoe backed up, suddenly afraid.

"I've watched you for a long time before we finally met. "Why do you hate your parents so much? They seem nice."

"They don't love me. They only pretend." It was the first time Zoe put into words the ugly thing she tried to smother with food.

Violet drifted over and said gently, "Don't be sad. I'm going to tell you a true story about a ghost that was possessed by a demon. It will horrify everyone who hears it and assure you of winning the writing competition." As Violet leaned over and began whispering in her ear, Zoe trembled, but the onset of one of her black moods instantly lifted and she started writing in the red spiral notebook.

***

The next time they met, Violet showed Zoe where she was buried. Her stone was located all the way in the back of the graveyard apart from the others.

"Why are you so far away?"

"Uncle Josiah insisted. He said I was cursed."

Zoe could just make out Violet's initials crudely carved into the stone and the date of her death, 1859. The ground was covered in dead leaves and weeds. It was such a lonely place. Zoe felt a lot of sympathy for Violet, but she had to get something off her chest.

"You were with me when I returned from school today. My parents should have seen you, but they looked right through you. And Marina Haskell was with me this morning when I met you in the woods. She didn't ask who you were either."

"Only you can see and hear me," Violet acknowledged.

Zoe couldn't hide her disappointment. "Are you sure you can't show yourself to others if you try really, really hard?"

"I'm sure. Why?"

"I was looking forward to seeing their faces when they realized you were a ghost, especially my parents. If I tell them about you, and they can't see you, they'll insist I see a shrink."

"I don't know what a shrink is, but most people don't believe in ghosts," Violet said.

"Am I the only one who can see you because I found the locket?"

"That's part of it," Violet agreed as she ran her long fingers through her tangled, blonde curls. "We share a bond."

Zoe was pleased. "What sort of bond?"

Violet stopped fussing with her hair. "Both of us

86

feel unloved and lonely. It drew us together."

For the first time in her life since Poppa died, Zoe felt special. How many people could claim a bond with a ghost?

***

School let out early on Halloween. Just as Violet predicted, Zoe's story won the writing contest. She wasn't surprised. Writing it down gave her nightmares. She impressed her parents, teacher, and the class. She felt truly happy. Violet joined her on the walk home.

"You won, didn't you?" Violet said.

"I did. Thank you."

"That's what friends are for."

It was freezing and the ground was hard with frost. As they walked past the houses, they could see people pouring bags of candy into huge, glass bowls, preparing for the night of the dead.

Candles flickered inside carved out pumpkins with jagged mouths. They leered from each window. Witches on brooms, white-sheeted ghosts, skeletons, and axe wielding monsters were placed strategically on porches, set to activate, releasing demonic screams and laughter as soon as the unwary took the first step.

"Want to have some fun," Violet asked.

"Sure."

"You stay hidden and watch."

Violet set the triggers off and rang the door bells. When a woman came to the door with a bowl of candy, Violet made the candy float in the air. Puzzled, the woman stepped onto the porch and looked around for the prankster. Violet poked her in the ribs with a stick and the woman screamed and dropped the bowl. Running inside, she shut and bolted the door. Zoe laughed so hard she cried.

"Do it again," Zoe said wiping her eyes.

Eventually, they tired of the game and returned to the cemetery.

"What do you do when you're not with me?" Zoe asked, chewing on a peanut butter cup, as Violet skipped over to a Maple tree and dived straight into it.

"Violet," Zoe shouted annoyed, "Stop showing off."

Disembodied laughter filled the air around them. Suddenly, Violet stood in front of Zoe who jumped.

"Sometimes I visit places I've never been before."

"Where? Tell me." Zoe insisted.

"India, China, Italy."

"How?" Zoe asked impressed.

"When you're a spirit, you just think about a place and you're there. Nothing can stop you going anywhere you want, even visiting the moon or hundreds of years in the past. It's so much fun."

Zoe was jealous. "But no one can see you."

"I also visit other ghosts and we play tricks on the living like we did today."

"Have you ever met my grandfather?" Zoe asked eagerly.

"Last night," Violet said playing with her hair.

"Did he ask about me?"

"I tried to talk to him, but he wouldn't listen. He doesn't realize he's dead and wanders around lost."

"Can't we do something?" Zoe wanted to hug Poppa one last time and tell him how much she loved him. Maybe she could help him to move on, wherever that was.

Violet stood on one foot, an inch in the air. "There is a way you could see him for a few hours." She hesitated. "But you might not want to."

"Tell me," Zoe demanded.

Violet whizzed over and sat down cross-legged on a pile of leaves in front of Zoe who joined her on the ground.

"Once a year on Halloween night, at the exact hour of midnight, the barrier between the spirit world and your world is weak. If you lay on the grave of a dead spirit who you feel connected to, like the bond we have, and you really want to, you can exchange your body for that of the dead person."

"You're making that up."

"It's true. I swear." Violet's face was serious.

"How many people have done it?"

"Not many," Violet admitted.

"It sounds dangerous," Zoe said shivering.

"It's perfectly safe. The spirits are called back to the spirit realm at dawn."

"What if I'm not back in time?"

"Your life force draws you back, silly."

"I don't' know," Zoe said frowning. "What if you like it here so much you don't want to leave?"

"Don't worry," Violet assured her, glancing at Zoe from beneath long lashes, "the dead have to obey the summons. We have no choice."

"It'll be freezing at midnight," Zoe complained.

"Bring some blankets. Your grandfather will be so happy to see you but," she added, "if we don't do it tonight, we'll have to wait another whole year. He might have moved on by then, or even worse, be so lost, he won't know who you are."

Zoe felt Violet had just stabbed her in the heart. She was still uneasy but Violet had never lied to her before. "I suppose we could try," she said. "You'd like to come back for a little while, wouldn't you, Violet?"

"More than anything," Violet said. Excitement made her eyes sparkle. "I could eat all the candy I want, take a hot bath and lie in a warm bed under a mound of down quilts."

Zoe thought Violet's desires rather tame after a hundred and fifty years, but it was none of her business. She would see Poppa again.

***

That night, while her parents were watching the eleven o'clock news, Zoe snuck out of the house. Under one arm, she carried a sleeping bag and a blanket. Violet joined her on her walk to the cemetery. Even though Zoe wore her down jacket and fur lined boots she was shaking with the cold and nerves.

"It's scary at night," Zoe said.

Violet giggled. "It's quiet that's all."

When they reached Violet's grave, they spread the sleeping bag on top. Zoe and Violet lay down and Zoe zipped the sleeping bag and blanket over the two of them.

"Do you think this will work?" Zoe whispered, torn between terror and doubt.

"Hush," Violet said.

Zoe told herself she was being very brave for Poppa.

The wind whipped dead leaves into her face. Zoe heard whispers and muted laughter. She watched in horror as spirits left their graves, floating through the trees, their ghostly skeletal faces grinning at her as they flew past.

"Violet," Zoe moaned. She was afraid.

A shadow passed over the moon and Violet rose up out of the sleeping bag, hovering above Zoe like a gleaming, silver wraith. Her blue eyes blazed. Zoe remembered the story of the demon ghost. The idea of the transfer of souls suddenly terrified her.

As she opened her mouth to say she changed her mind, Violet blew a white, freezing cold, gossamer breath into Zoe's nose and mouth, numbing her. Zoe discovered she couldn't move. She felt a snap at the back of her skull and a sucking motion as a soft, pearly light floated out through her nose, mouth, ears, and eyes to mingle with Violet's incandescent one. The two souls twisted and turned as though wrestling until one broke free.

Gasping, Violet fell back. She sat up, unzipped the sleeping bag, and stood up. Examining her body, she realized she was solid. She watched as Zoe's startled ghost surveyed her transparent limbs in horror and vanished like a wisp of fog.

Violet grabbed the gold locket Zoe left behind and called out "Enjoy yourself Zoe. I will." Laughing, she skipped away, leaving the blanket and sleeping bag behind.

***

The next morning, Zoe came down to breakfast. Her mother was drinking coffee. Her father poured milk over his oatmeal. "Good morning, mom" she said hugging Trudy who stared at her in surprise.

"Toast," her father asked.

Zoe sat down. "Cereal and fruit, please and skim milk. Today I go on a diet."

Trudy and Frank exchanged looks of amazement, followed by delight which they quickly hid.

A locket fell out of her sweater and Zoe quickly tucked it back inside as she smiled at her mother. "Can you take me shopping today? I want to buy some pretty clothes."

"I'll drive you to the Rockingham Mall after breakfast and pick you up in two hours. Is that enough time?"

"Actually, Zoe said, "I was hoping you'd come with me and help me choose."

"If you'd like," Trudy said, so stunned she spilled coffee all over her Benetton sweater.

A terrible howl reverberated through the house. The shutters banged open and shut.

Zoe's ghost stood beside Frank screaming.

"Look at me."

Frank shivered. "Turn up the heat. And what is

91

that awful sound?"

"Just the wind, daddy. Just the wind," Violet said softly as she sipped her orange juice.

"The Haunted that Still Haunts" by Sonali Roy

**The supernatural is the natural
not yet understood.**

— **Elbert Hubbard, 1856-1915, American writer**

**Ghosts were created when
the first man awoke in the night.**

— **James Barrie, 1860-1937, English writer**

Alone
Alexis Child

I am a pale ghost. Lost, wandering
Chasing whims and shadows
Hiding in dark places
Now free of tooth and flesh
Everything I once imagined

I reach with no arms
And stand with no legs
I am the breeze on windless nights
That will take away your breath

To most, I am faceless, nameless
And bear no threat
In the distance just a silhouette
That no one notices
A ghost you know exists but don't believe
A ghost that haunts itself in this dark dream
Say you'll remember me

The Inner Eye Opening
Daniel R. Robichaud

The headaches began on the thirteenth day of his two weeks on, one week off shift. Gunther Fast was in the middle of a mud tank spot weld when his head suddenly felt like it was going to come apart. The first rule of hot work was never put yourself or another person in danger. Instead of pushing through the pain to finish up, he killed the torch and hobbled away in search of aspirin. He wound up in the company trailer. Fletcher Lansdale fetched Advil from his medical kit, and Gunther dry swallowed two blue tablets before any water was forthcoming.

"Why'd you stop, G-man?" Toby asked. The barrel chested fellow with the pipsqueak's voice was the company man and his log was showing Non-Productive Time, the biggest no-no in any field report. Taking one look at Gunther, he then asked, "You need a chair or something, hoss?"

"Yeah." Gunther sat down before he fell over.

Outside the trailer's window, the sunshine made the oil patch glow with the dreadful red-brown color of old blood. Place looked like it was viewed through the rancid meat of last week's blood oranges. People ran, and though he could not hear them their mouths opened in hollers. Then, a guy with a black moustache and no hardhat raced to the trailer's window, banging on the glass. Words suddenly became audible: "The power pack's redlining. It's gone blow!"

When he blinked, the vision vanished.

The company man's face pinched like someone'd squeezed out the wettest, juiciest fart imaginable. He muttered something about finding a relief welder to finish up and then hurried on his way.

Soon after the trailer door banged shut, Lansdale held up fingers, asking how many Gunther could see. He checked the spot welder's pulse. He tested Gunther's eyes with a penlight. As the glowing tip swept left and right, the welder swooned. Lansdale caught him by the arm, and Gunther shivered as a new sight filled his vision, some faraway place ...

A small house on a modest patch of land, swept white with fresh snow. A car eased out of a garage and down the ice crusted drive toward the road but didn't make it further than midway. With a rev and rub of wheels without traction, the car careened out of control. Fishtailed into a boulder. A loud crunch stopped the car dead. The driver's door kicked open and a slim shape emerged to inspect the damage. The man set foot wrong and went down hard, landing with a bone snapping crunch. He lay there, wheezing as the next wave of snow drifted down. Dr. Fletcher Lansdale lay on his busted back, weakly calling a woman's name. His arms pinwheeled. His leg did not even twitch.

"The hell you say," Lansdale muttered, as Gunther's vision swam back to the trailer's interior.

Had Gunther said something? "I'll be all right, Doc." Truth be told, his head felt like someone was whacking a hatchet against his crown, eager to split the skull like a melon.

"Your pupils are going crazy," Lansdale said. "You on something? Speed? Methamphetamines to keep you going?"

"That's a firing offense."

"So it is," Lansdale agreed. "I know you're a dependable guy. But anyone can slip."

"I don't take drugs."

Lansdale pursed his lips. "You need a hospital, man. I'm making the call."

"For a headache?"

"No. Your . . . vitals are concerning me. Could be serious."

"It's a headache!"

"Could be a stroke," Lansdale said. "Could be onset of diabetic shock."

"Dia— Doc, you know I'm not diabetic."

"Could be a bunch of different things, Gunther. You need to be checked out."

"But—"

"No buts. I said I'm making the call. You sit right there and wait. Someone'll drive you back to the Yard, where a helicopter'll be waiting."

"*Helicopter?*"

The door banged shut behind Lansdale. Gunther could not stand up to follow the doc if he'd wanted to. Any time he shifted his posture, his head throbbed worse. When he tried to stand up, his vision blanked out.

Heart racing a mile a minute, Gunther dropped back into the seat. Seconds later, his vision returned. Head throbbed all the worse.

Through the wall, Gunther heard a snippet of conversation. One man said, "There's no way anyone could've guessed that Cat's readout was broken. They test these things before deployment, don't they? But here comes company man, demanding a manual test. Damn lucky. The power packs could've gone up and took out half the camp." Another man said, "It wasn't Toby at all. Hear it was Gunther Fast made the call. He been babbling a bunch today. They stopped him working, too." The first man asked, "How's he supposed to know something like that?" Before the second man could answer, the conversation moved on, but Gunther's soul was as cold as Alaska's North Slope.

Lansdale returned with that weightlifting Swede Tom Bullens. "Tom here's gonna take you back to the

Yard."

Tom came in all friendly like, but his manner betrayed wariness. *You been hearing the guys talk about me, Tom?* Gunther could not ask that, so he asked, "How bad do I look?"

Never one to mince words or pussyfoot around, Lansdale drew a breath, let it out, and then explained: "Like a man who died, got hisself buried, and then dug up."

"Let's get this show on the road," Tom said, recovering enough spine to help Gunther along.

Gunther leaned on the man because his knees threatened to give. "This is one hell of a headache."

"I'll make sure the chopper's there to meet you," Lansdale said. "You go on and get checked out. We'll see you soon."

The Swede led Gunther to the site's perimeter where the trucks waited, engines grumbling. Tom's ride was a beat to hell, white company pickup with the red letter-H logo on the side. Tom opened the door, guided Gunther in, and closed the door behind him. Gunther fiddled with getting the seatbelt buckled while Tom hurried to the driver's side.

A line of men watched Gunther's progress, and now they were looking at him through the windshield. Gunther caught more than a little concern in their expressions. They were generally good guys, workhorses. He offered them a weak wave of the hand. Some of his pals waved back. Then, Tom pulled out of camp and onto the rough and rutted dirt trail the site called a road, hustling the forty miles to the Yard.

A fair-haired woman was laid out in a bed, and a man sat alongside her holding her hand. Machines waited around her, ready to catch the first trace of her body trying to shut down. The machines could do nothing, of course, should she choose to eject the mortal shell. The man looked back when someone called from the door, and though his face was distorted by suffering and grief, it was Tom Bullens. The woman was not old enough to be his mother. A wife, then. Sister? A daughter, maybe. So hard to tell because she was so wizened.

Gunther passed out for much of the twenty-minute drive. He came around to find the truck stopped outside the Yard between Monahans and Midland-Odessa, waiting for the guard to process them through.

"Hey there, Guns," the Swede said. "How you doing?"

"Groggy."

"How's the head?

"Little better." It was as bad as before. Maybe worse.

"You were crying," Tom said.

"Was I?"

Tom nodded. "Crying *out*, I mean. Talking in your sleep. A little unnerving."

Gunther said nothing.

"The magnetic whatever on my ID is kaput. They have to run me every time I come here." Tom chuckled. "And I come here for parts all the damned time."

His laugh seemed a little forced.

The guard returned and handed Tom back his ID. Then he hit a button. The gate opened and he waved them in.

Tom didn't stare at his passenger, but Gunther saw the way his eyes shifted over from time to time, gauging him.

"Did I say anything entertaining?" Gunther asked.

"Entertaining?"

"Yeah. I had a college roommate. Used to nap or fall asleep and then talk. You could ask him questions, he'd answer them. Not remember anything when he woke up. Fun party trick."

"Well, I don't know about that," the Swede said. "But you were crying, like I said. Calling out. You said somethings didn't make sense. Most of the time, you made dinosaur calls."

"Made whatnow?"

"You know," Tom said. He made a sound that started high up and then went low. An eerie kind of noise, not too different from one of those lighthouse horns old timers used to warn boats away from rocks during fog.

"I don't remember making such a noise," Gunther admitted.

In his dream, the Tom sitting beside the woman made a sound like the driver described. But that was a dream, nothing he said aloud. He'd know if he cried out.

"Wouldn't expect you to," Tom said. "You were out like a light."

As Lansdale promised, a helicopter waited on the landing pad over by Building Q. Tom drove him over, and a trio of medics met him, got his information, checked off their documentation and loaded him onto a stretcher.

The rotors whipped around and around, making that tell-tale fwap-fwap-fwap*fwapfwap*. Then, the whirlybird rose into the air, carrying him on to the Odessa Medical Center. The medic responsible for monitoring him spent an inordinate amount of time wiping his gloves on alcohol swab towelettes, which was more than just some quirky behavior. Made Gunther wonder if he was contagious.

They were still fifteen minutes from the hospital when the world went away once more, replaced by somewhere else.

His neighbors, John and Muriel Talbot, were

99

loading up the truck with their daughter's furniture and bags, readying her for the move into the dorms. She was super geeked to be getting out of San Marcos and off to Austin to live on campus in The Big City even though Austin was at most an hour's drive from her parents' house. Kids got some funny ideas sometimes . . . Mostly, he expected she was happy to get away from her parents for a while. They were just like the ride he was still inside, hovering around her, warning and expecting her to fail. Jenna was a smart kid, and she could use some slack. A little space. Just ask her . . .

The image shifted from the family packing her up for her freshman semester to the truck rolling along on the highway, heading north to the University of Texas. As they rode along, an oncoming eighteen wheeler drifted across the yellow line. The driver of that big fella bobbed his head up, and the truck wove to its proper lane. Guy was exhausted, as they sometimes were. Delirium was a danger.

The Talbot pickup tried to get right, but a car in the slow lane carried along oblivious. As John's truck neared the semi, entering the point of no return, the eighteen wheeler's driver dropped his head again and the big rig veered once more across the line at just the wrong time . . . John pulled to the right, but his Ford truck clipped the semi's bumper.

That brush ripped off his front quarter panel, crumpled the driver's side and sheared off the hood release. Steel flapped up and tore free, smashing the windshield and blinding the driver. As Talbot fished stuff out of his eyes, the wheel turned out of control, first finishing the right hand turn until it rebounded off the neighboring car and then veering to the left. Jenna screamed, and the airbag popped, trying to cushion her. The real damage was yet to come and inescapable. The truck nosed right into the gap between the semi's cargo trailer, which blew out Talbot's tires and shoved the Talbot truck's nose down into the pavement just in time for the trailer's rear set of wheels to roll over Austin-bound pickup truck. Those rear wheels crashed into the passenger side quarter panel, squeezing the engine block through the thin steel barrier and into the driver and passenger's compartment. The height those wheels rose to compared to the rest of the truck soon surpassed a critical amount. The truck's trailer rolled first, going over almost in slow motion and then pulling the cab with it. In the end, it was like a kid's Tonka truck, landing on its side and sawing grooves through asphalt and the overgrown shoulder, before plowing down into the rainwater ditches and then coming to an abrupt stop. The trailer jackknifed around, swinging like the hand of an insanely large analog clock, sweeping still more vehicles off the road, including a Lowe's truck carrying a few dozen Blue Rhino propane cannisters. The abundant sparks set those off and the truck exploded, spewing flames thirty feet into the air. Fires spread, between other cars and the jackknifed trailer, too. The refrigerated pig carcasses it carried scattered across the road, ablaze and filling the air with the stench of cooked flesh.

In the Talbot family truck. Jenna was not moving, not trying to get her seatbelt unfastened, not trying to rouse her father. Something was wrong with her insides. All she could do was stare, blink, cry, and bleed. A rolling pig carcass bounced off her dad's side of the pickup truck. Those flames already dangerously close to fluids pumping out of the destroyed pickup truck's engine. In the next few seconds, they would catch. She was going to burn, as well. Eighteen, looking forward to freedom, and dead on the highway not six miles from home . . .

When Gunther came to, the paramedics were

gone and with them the chopper. Gunther was on an uncomfortable bed, strapped to a gurney. A kind faced, auburn haired woman in a white coat appeared over him, asking if he could understand her. When he said he could and demanded to know who she was, she beamed a good bedside manner smile. "I'm Doctor—"

"Benedetta?" he asked. "I think I heard someone say Benedetta?"

Her smile faltered. "That was my maiden name. I'm Rosa Stross, now. You're having an interesting variety of symptoms, Mr. Fast. Would you mind answering a few questions?"

"I don't understand," he said. "But I think I need a phone. I need to call my neighbor in San Marcos—"

The dream had been far too lucid to be a dream. Too compelling. Too *real*. "I need a phone—"

"Another one of your experiences?" she asked, surprisingly blasé.

"Huh?"

"I hesitate to call them visions, but a few of the others are already dubbing them something like that. Saying you're a prophet of some kind." Her smile was conciliatory. "They come close and you speak their names out loud, even though they've never introduced themselves. Even though you're asleep. How can that be?"

"I don't know what you're talking about. I've never had anything like that happen to me before."

She said, "It just happened, didn't it?"

"Did it?"

"You knew my maiden name," Dr. Stross said.

"I must've heard someone—"

"Perhaps," she agreed.

"You don't think so," he said. "Lord my head aches."

"When did this start."

"Work today." Was it today? "I just came in, right?"

She nodded. "Did this start at your company yard?"

He shook his head, but the motion sent streams of agony running through his spine and skull. "Not Yard," he muttered. "Field."

"The oil patch?"

"Yes, ma'am. I was doing hot work on a mud tank."

"Hot work. That's welding?"

"Yes, ma'am."

"Wearing all the required equipment?"

She meant personal protective equipment. "Yes, ma'am." But his PPE had not been the best. Loose fits because whoever used the mask before had stretched out the band. The gloves were a little thin. He could smell the dregs of diesel-based mud, polluted with whatever cuttings bypassed the filtration methods and wound up in the tank. He hadn't thought much of it at the time, but the smell had been kicking off his headache. It should not have worked its way into his head so fast. He'd worked in worse conditions without incident.

"All it takes is one slipup," she said, finishing the thought he'd half-articulated in his skull. "And your life changes forever."

"I think something's wrong with my head," Gunther said. "I think I might be . . . might be going crazy. Seeing things that aren't real. That don't make a lot of sense to me."

"But what you're seeing is making sense to the people you tell it to."

Gunther did not know what to say.

"Were you out at Anadarko 42 by chance?" Dr. Stross asked.

"How did you know?"

103

"That's why I was called in on your case," she said. "There's something about that place, which induces a specific set of symptoms. If you only started contracting the symptoms today, then the damage might not be extensive."

"Damage?"

Her expression turned grave. "I'm not going to deceive you. We've had a couple of incurable patients. The experiences become all consuming, and their understanding of the world is restricted. Blasts of lucidity between bouts of . . . of unreality."

What was she talking about? How could he have sustained *damage* from loose PPE on hot work? The biggest danger in the field was H_2S leaking out of the hole, and that didn't give you hallucinations, it killed you stone dead in seconds. There was nothing like what she was saying. No one told him about anything like this. The company was supposed to post . . . to prepare . . . to warn its people of potential threats and hazards.

"I haven't heard anything about what you're referring to."

She shrugged. "I doubt the company is mentioning this. But they tend to cycle through different service providers, don't they? Over time, I mean. One person unexpectedly leaving a site during the course of a job? It's not unheard of."

Gunther supposed it was not. "My headache's less, though."

"Which is a good sign. I really don't want another special case winding up in the incurable ward."

"The whatnow?"

"Am I saying something right now? Or just thinking it?"

He studied her mouth, which was not moving. The words were still audible. Though he wondered if they appeared inside his skull would he know the difference? "You're not like any doctor I've ever met," he said.

Thank goodness her mouth moved and even formed the right word combinations when she said, "Because I'm not."

"*You're not a doctor?*"

"Not like any one you've ever met before." Dr. Stross sat down next to his bed. "In fact, I'm an MD/PhD. A combination that doesn't run rampant through hospitals in west Texas. I'm a research driven operator, with three RO1s from the National Institutes of Health. I specialize in studying the victims of Anadarko 42."

"If it's such a hotbed, why not study the site itself?"

"I petitioned to do just that, but the company declined my offer. They are a working site, as you know, and my presence could interfere with quotas or production levels or whatever metric they use."

"But if there's something hurting people—"

"Well, you and I both know that no company is going to bend over backward to solve a problem that doesn't matter to the bottom line," she said. "The question is how many people get hurt, and how likely lawsuits are, and how much can be lost to an average lawsuit. This kind of a scenario is the lowest of the low risk ones, at least until the company sees a surge."

Gunther did not like that term. It made his headache flare up into worse regions—was that even possible? Could the thoughts his mind evoked trigger some kind of biological response? He half-recalled the term psychosomatic and how it once related to soldiers whose brains made their hands not work when they were too terrified to go into battle. He also recalled the opposite effect, phantom limbs for amputees who could still *feel* their missing arms or legs. The mind was a powerful little computer, better than any device mankind could manufacture, and it could accomplish things that were nothing short of miraculous.

"So, what's happening?" Gunther asked. "Specifically?"

"Specifically," she repeated the word, "I do not have enough evidence to support my hypothesis."

"And what is your hypothesis?"

"A contagion of some sort located in Anadarko 42 is causing a rapid development of dormant psychokinetic and psychological abilities in sensitized subjects."

"Sensitized?"

"Are you familiar with neurotransmitters?"

"Not even a little."

Dr. Stross pursed her lips. "Well, suffice to say the brain is one big generator. It is a bio-electrical module that controls everything we see and hear, but it is also a kind of radio. The neurons generate these molecules that bridge the synapses, the gaps between them, carrying messages from one to the next to the next. Kind of like a Pony Express darting between the cells in our heads. My studies have shown that the makeup of these molecules is not uniform. Nothing in biology is uniform, when you pay attention to the smallest parts that make up an organism. That's why side effects for medications can vary so much: different people's makeups will respond differently to chemicals." She sighed and sat down. "You and some other folks have neurotransmitters that utilize a similar makeup so as to be receptive to interference from the unknown source. Neural pathways are being reshaped, the transmitters are being repurposed, and your brain is being altered."

"My brain is broken?"

"In the most general sense," she said. "In that it's

changed from what it was before your exposure to the mystery source."

"Can you fix it? Can my brain get *repaired?*"

She did not say anything for almost three seconds, and in that time he felt his terrors escalating to outrageous levels. Then, Dr. Stross said, "The brain is a resilient machine, a beautiful and clever organ. If those pathways can be amended, it will do so on its own. There is no kind of procedure that can do the work your brain is doing."

"What are the chances that I'll be normal?"

"Well, your exposure was less than any of the other patients—"

"And how many of them made a recovery?"

"A full recovery?"

"Or partial. Any kind of progress." Gunther's head hurt so much he had to close his eyes and squeeze the bridge of his nose between thumb and forefinger.

"Well, we've never had a full recovery," Dr. Stross said. "But we've had several partial recoveries. In six of the dozen patients I've seen."

"That's fifty percent!" he said. Terrible odds but not hopeless ones. He could flip a coin—

"But none of our patients has returned to a level of functionality that would allow them to live and work in the normal world."

"Hopeless cases."

"Not hopeless," she emphasized. "There's always —"

"I'm going to wind up in a rubber room? Because my PPE didn't fit right?"

"The rooms are not rubber," she said, as though this were the most important correction to make in his assumptions. "But there's no guarantee you'll need confinement. You had a limited dose, so there's still a—"

"Still a chance I can live in my house? Next to my

neighbors?" The Talbots, he realized he still needed to talk to them. "I want that phone. There's a call I must make."

"There are a lot of calls," she said. "And you've made several of them. A nurse here won't be going to Drillers on Saturday because you said she would be involved in a hit and run accident in the parking lot. There's a candy striper who's not going to cut out early tonight, the way she'd planned, because a car's going to run a red light, swerve out of the way of a woman in the crosswalk, plow into a telephone pole, which will come smashing down on her Prius. There's a doctor who's going to take his Lipitor every day instead of just the days when he remembers because his granddaughter is going to get hit with a big dose of despair when she turns eighteen—that's ten years from now—and grapple with feelings she can't talk to her parents about but that she *could* talk to him about. A lot of people have come into contact with you. People you never realized you were touching. But you have touched them."

Gunther did not know what to say. "I don't remember any of . . . of that."

She shrugged. "You're conscious, now. You're aware, now. You weren't before. That's improvement I've seldom seen. And your visions are slowing. There was a rush of them in the beginning. But now, a trickle. You haven't had one as long as we've been talking, right?"

Not since the one about the Talbots, in fact. Fifteen, almost twenty minutes ago?

"I take your silence as an affirmation."

"So, I sit here and hope they stop altogether? How long will that—"

Dr. Stross held up her hands, but he already knew she would.

"And why am I seeing tragedies? Why not

108

something useful?"

"Like the Powerball numbers?" she asked.

"Well, yeah."

"Because whatever you got exposed to, it seems to be concerned with pain and suffering. Specifically with *alleviating* it. Or, alternative theory, the impact its presence has on you predisposes you toward witnessing pain and suffering, and you are alleviating it subconsciously." She sighed. "There's so much I don't know and so much I want to learn."

A pretty redheaded nurse arrived with pain medications. The way she looked at him, he felt like a bug on a slide about to be stuck into a microscope.

He popped the medication and downed the cup of water, and the redhead hustled out of the room. Gunther asked, "What did I say to her?"

"Nothing," Dr. Stross said. "But people are talking."

"So, they think I'm a freak?"

"Most of them think you've been touched by God or something similar. They are all afraid of what you'll tell them, but at the same time they all want to talk to you for just a minute. If you say everything's going to be all right, then they will listen. But if you say something terrible is going to happen, then they'll wrack their brains trying to figure out how to bypass it."

He did not know what to say to that, so he just sulked in bed. A blackout came over him, but he did not realize it until he saw how the clock advanced fifteen minutes between blinking his eyes. Dr. Stross was concerned, but still seated.

"Well," she said. "Are you back?"

"I never left," Gunther replied, but was that true? He had the sense of being . . . elsewhere for a moment. He couldn't be here because time got away from him. In that heartbeat between closing his eyes and opening them again, he must've been somewhere far from here.

"So you say now."

"What happened? Did I tell you about your future?"

She shook her head. "You . . . the thing that opened up your inner eye. It reached through you, spoke to me."

"What did it say?"

"You said you were buried in the oil field. That's what you told me. Buried there and waiting for someone to find you, bring you up, deliver you to the surface. The well drilling machines passed right on by because you were not precious. In time, they would move on and then I would go to free you." Tears filled her eyes.

"I don't know what to say, Dr. Stross."

"It is I who should say something. *Thank you.* You gave me something precious, Gunther. You gave me access to something I'd been having trouble holding onto. You gave me hope. In ten years, fifteen, I will have more answers. Whatever is out there, it doesn't mean us harm. It doesn't mean to hinder. It's been buried a long while, and it's aware of the effect it has, and every single person it harms is pain it feels too."

"What is it? Where did it come from? Outer space?"

"I don't know," Dr. Stross said. "It did not specify, but to tell me that answers were in the waiting. That I would have them in ten or fifteen years."

"Or sooner, if we can get Anadarko off that patch."

She laughed. "They won't go. And when the wells run dry, there will be some kind of new stimulus. The next technological leap from frac. Nanotechnology or something. Ten years. Fifteen at most? Then, 42 will be bone dry, no longer interesting for the bottom line.

Then, I will find my answers."

"And did the . . . did the thing that was inside me? Did it say anything about me?"

"Your inner eye is open. In time, given patience and practice, you can learn to see with it and live with it, but . . . I get the feeling doing so won't be easy. A spiritual equivalent of the physical therapy. But I'm here to help you, Mr. Fast. It will be my pleasure to help you because . . ."

"Because you need me, huh, Doc?" he asked. "Because you need me in ten or fifteen years to find the buried . . ." What had she called it? The origin? No. "The source. You need me to help you locate the buried source."

She nodded. "I'm not often so mercenary."

He laughed. "Sounds like we're going to have plenty of time to get to know one another."

"Worlds enough and time," she said, which sounded too fancy to be spontaneous. "Maybe we'll get to know ourselves, too."

The pain pills kicked in and the ache in Gunther Fast's skull ebbed away. Exhaustion reached up to grab onto him, easing him down into that place overflowing with dreams and visions that might not come true.

Seeing his eyelids drooping, Dr. Stross patted his hand. "Rest up, Mr. Fast. I won't be far when you wake."

He was happy for that. Even after his recent blackout, she did not look at him like he was going to grow a second head. Gunther did not want to feel like a freak or a prophet, a devil or a savior. And since his headaches began, she was the one person who managed not to look at him with awe, wonder, or terror. If there was someone he was looking forward to seeing, it was her.

Sleep overtook him, but the eye that had opened

111

inside of him remained wide and staring, beholding past, present, and the many future possibilities.

"Abandoned" by Sonali Roy

House
Lynn White

It was hardly a gingerbread house.
Only the roof was gingerbread colour.
We thought the old woman living there was a witch.
Later we didn't believe in witches
and we knew she was no more a witch
than the raindrops
hanging from the trees
were really diamonds,
though she said that they were.
Now the house stands empty and derelict
and we know no one has lived there for centuries.
Only the raindrops remain
frozen in time
hard as diamonds
just as she said they were.

Words: *Eric Esquivel; Art: Ryan Cody*

Article

Severed Heads And Omens Of Death:
The Horror Origins Of Halloween
Gary Davis

Preface

The article below is necessarily speculative. The intent here is not to present a broad or recent history of Halloween, which has already been done by many writers; (see, for example, *Trick or Treat: A History of Halloween* (2012) and *The Halloween Encyclopedia* (2003, 2011), both by Lisa Morton). Instead, the objective is to identify likely or plausible horrific elements of belief, culture and social behavior contributing to the origin and character of Halloween in the distant past. This past almost certainly extends into prehistoric ages which produced no indigenous written records. Thus, one is obliged to rely on uncertain inferences made from archaeological remains—buildings, earthworks, artifacts, skeletons, and preserved "bog bodies"—the latter exhibiting their own horrific features. In some cases, written records from neighboring literate societies are available. One can also glean information from stories, myths and legends handed down orally across countless generations; many of these were finally committed to writing during the Middle Ages.

The Halloween of today is conventionally encapsulated within the cheery, door-to-door exclamation of kids: "Trick-or-treat!" Here we do not go in search of "fun-size" treats or other candy. We dust off the ancient horrors lying behind the "trick".

***

Probably no Western holiday has shapeshifted

down through the years as much as Halloween. The way it is commonly celebrated nowadays is quite different from celebrations just a few generations ago. And there are greater differences the further one recedes back in time, to the Middle Ages, ancient history and the misty depths of prehistoric eras. This mutability of Halloween celebrations is in fact a major reason for the holiday's continued survival across many centuries; it is incredibly adaptable.

As the word "shapeshifting" implies, the outward form or practical content of Halloween activities has significantly changed over time. There is a more consistent inner core of belief, myth and legend, however, that has been passed down from distant eras. This core is derived from the ancient culture of the Celts living in Ireland, Scotland and elsewhere in the British Isles. The Celts lived in intimate contact with dangerous and unpredictable forces of both man and nature. There was necessarily a realm of "supernature" that always hovered nearby, sensed if not seen.

The supernatural realm of the early Celts was one of threat, trickery and, by modern standards, outright horror. It was especially permeable and open to contact with living humans during the transition from predominantly warm to predominantly cold weather marked by the Celtic new year celebration, called Samhain ("sow-in") in ancient Ireland (began October 31-November 1). This was a time when crops were being harvested, and cattle and other domestic animals were brought home from upland pastures; many of the animals were then slaughtered for winter provisions.

A successful harvest was an occasion for celebration at Samhain, including political/religious assemblies, feasting and bonfires. Still, a specter of death lurked in the background at this time of year.

The temperature was colder. Dead leaves fell from the trees. The life-giving Sun remained below the horizon for longer and longer periods; people wondered if it would return. The landscape took on a barren look. In some years, there was a likelihood of famine if the harvest fell short; there was a threat of damage from fierce winter storms. Warfare with hostile neighboring clans was always a possibility.

The noted Iron Age and Celtic scholar, Miranda Aldhouse-Green, has some strong words to say about Samhain:

> The most sinister festival was Samhain at the end of October, a dangerous and liminal event that marked the end of the old year and the beginning of the new. It was a period when time was in abeyance and the barriers between the spirits, the dead and living people were temporarily dissolved (Miranda Aldhouse-Green, *Bog Bodies Uncovered: Solving Europe's Ancient Mystery*, 2015, p. 193).

Faced with so many uncertainties and dangers, the ancient Celts engaged with the supernatural realm in order to divine the future. Omens of death, such as a raven spotted on the roof of one's house, could appear at this time. Fortune-telling games eventually became a staple feature of Halloween celebrations over the centuries; (see, for example, Ruth Edna Kelley, *The Book of Hallowe'en*, 1919; Robert Burns, "*Hallowe'en*" (poem), 1785).

The Celts populated their supernatural domain with a great many beings—deities, fairies and spirits of the dead. Supposed fairy "sightings", at any time of year, have occurred in Ireland and elsewhere in the British Isles into the 20th century. They were particularly common, and often feared, in the 1600s and earlier, before the Age of Enlightenment. Fairy battles tended to occur on Samhain. (Richard Sugg, *Fairies: A Dangerous History*, 2018).

Spirits of the dead included one's ancestors and enemies killed in battle. Celtic warriors often severed the heads of dead enemy warriors and kept the skulls as trophies in their houses (according to the ancient Greek geographer Posidonius (1st century BCE); numerous decapitated skulls have been dug up at riverine sites in the area of ancient Londinium, as well as headless skeletons in France). Since the spirit cr soul was believed to reside in the head, control of an enemy's head could provide protection against his vengeful ghost, which might wander abroad when the restless underworld opened up on Samhain Eve.

While not proven, there is a distinct possibility that the Halloween Jack-o'-Lantern evolved in tandem with the Celtic severed head trophy. The candle inside the lantern represented the still living spirit of the deceased. Early Irish Samhain lanterns were often made from turnips and rutabagas (*pumkinnook.com*). Turnips seem to be shaped more like a human head than the later pumpkin lantern. On Samhain Eve, the early Jack-o'-Lantern probably served a dual purpose: 1) to guide the spirits of one's ancestors back to their family dwelling for a friendly visit and food treats, and 2) to ward or scare off the potentially dangerous and vengeful ghosts of one's enemies.

Certain natural phenomena took on an extra dimension of forbidding supernatural meaning, especially at Samhain. An example is the ghost or night lights called "will o' the wisp" (also "fairy lights", "fool's fire"), caused by the natural combustion of decaying plant material and marsh gas in swamps. These eerie lights could lure travelers to their doom, drowning them in deep swamp water. In Wales, people believed that the will o' the wisp was "too bad to go into heaven and too clever to be taken into hell." This statement sounds a lot like the well-known legend of Stingy Jack and the first Jack-o'-Lantern. Again, there are horror origins to Halloween if one looks deeply back in time (Matt Soniak, "What's the Origin of Jack-o'-Lanterns," *mentalfloss.com*, 2012; Richard Sugg, *Fairies: A Dangerous History*, 2018).

Were sacrifices performed on Samhain? The answer is probably "yes", given the need for divination and the propitiation of a dangerously open underworld at this time of year. Animals brought down from pasture would have been readily available. Was human sacrifice also practiced by the Celts on Samhain? The answer to this question will likely never be known. The possibility cannot be ruled out entirely, based on the evidence of bog body "rituals", severed heads, and the statements of Greek and Roman writers. Julius Caesar, for example, made note of human sacrifices at Celtic festivals. The writings of most Classical authors, however, were generally distorted by political and cultural prejudices; the Celts to them were nothing more than dangerous "barbarians".

Regarding the bog body deaths, Miranda Aldhouse-Green states: "The weight of evidence for religious involvement strongly indicates that sacrificial rites were the main reason for the Iron Age European bog killings." Many of the bog body victims suffered a curious amount of overkill, even a three-fold death, that is inconsistent with a purely "legal" execution or death in battle. The British Lindow Man, for example, was strangled, received a throat slice and two blows to the head. Based on analysis of digestive remains, the bog body victims were generally killed in either wintertime or late summer to early autumn (pp. 175, 194), thus framing the period around Samhain and leaving open Samhain as at least a possible date for some of these killings (Miranda Aldhouse-Green, *Bog Bodies Uncovered: Solving Europe's Ancient Mystery*, 2015, pp. 191; 175, 194; Colm, "New Bog Body Found in Rossan, Co. Meath," *Irish Archaeology*, irisharchaeology.ie, September 16, 2014).

Many people recall bobbing for apples in a tub of water during Halloween parties when they were kids. Further back in time, apples were a major element in Halloween fortune-telling games. The tub of water used in apple-bobbing, however, evokes a more sinister past. Ancient Celtic legends include human sacrifices done by drowning in large cauldrons, which were significant ritual artifacts in their culture. Such a sacrifice may be shown on the famous Gundestrup Cauldron. These sacrifices were generally done in honor of the god Teutates (called Dispater by the Romans). There are legends of Irish kings who died by drowning in a basin.

> "...the sacrifice by asphyxiation in the cauldron appears to be attached to the feast of Samain (Samhain), the Celtic New Year..." (Jean Markale, *The Celts: Uncovering the Mythic and Historic Origins of Western Culture*, Rochester, Vermont: Inner Traditions International, 1993 (first published in Paris, France, 1976), pp. 231, 233).

How far back in time does Samhain go? It probably dates at least to the final prehistoric era of Celtic Europe, the Iron Age of the 1st millennium BCE, prior to the partial Roman conquest of Britain in the 1st century AD. (Most of the European bog bodies, including several found in Ireland, Old

Croghan Man and Clonycavan Man—both mutilated in various ways—have been radiocarbon dated to the second half of the 1st millennium BCE.) However, Celtic languages along the Atlantic seaboard—and perhaps the origins of Celtic culture—may go back much further, to the fifth millennium BCE. Another hypothesis is that proto-Celtic culture dates to the Bell Beaker era of the Bronze Age, during the third to second millenniums BCE.

Archaeology magazine has reported interesting evidence of an advanced age for Celtic ritual culture in Ireland:

> At the site of Tlachtga, on the Hill of Ward in County Meath—the site of circular earthworks associated with Samhain, the Celtic festival that gave birth to Halloween—recent remote sensing work has revealed three phases of construction, suggesting a long and varied ritual history that could go back more than 4,000 years ("World Roundup," *Archaeology,* September/October, 2014, p. 20).

Whatever actual horrors thrived during ancient Celtic Samhain, the direct fear and terror they inspired are long gone. Contemporary Halloween culture has preserved them as a distant collective memory, or half-memory. "Trick-or-treat!"

Article

Psychedelics and the Paranormal
R.D. Hayes

During the late 1940s through the 1960s, classically psychedelic drugs like LSD, mescaline, and psilocybin were used medically to great effect for mental conditions ranging from depression to addiction. As early as 1934, alcoholic Bill Wilson had visions under treatment with belladonna, a highly toxic hallucinogenic drug derived from the deadly nightshade plant. Wilson would go on to found the staunchly abstinence-only twelve-step program Alcoholics Anonymous. In 1956, Wilson had a mystical experience under the influence of LSD that ended his symptoms of depression. Such outside help was seen as a mark against his organization's effectiveness, and he was silenced.

> Stephen Ross, Director of NYU Langone's Health Psychedelic Medicine Research and Training Program, explains: "[In A.A.] you certainly can't be on morphine or methadone. There's this attitude that all drugs are bad, except you can have as many cigarettes and as much caffeine and as many doughnuts as you want."

After decades of being on the Drug Enforcement Agency's Schedule 1, psychedelics are once again are being used in medical research funded by the National Institutes of Health here in the United States, and in countries around the world. Drugs of different structure but similar effects, including ketamine and MDMA ("Ecstasy") are also being investigated. In fact, MDMA is likely to be the first approved, specifically for treating Post Traumatic Stress Disorder, and soon after for other anxiety disorders.

Not all of these drugs are hallucinogenic in the same way. For instance, LSD is famous for vivid visual and auditory hallucinations, which often touch upon deep psychological issues in a metaphorical way, while MDMA allows people to relive memories from inside a comfortable cocoon of positive emotion, where those memories cannot cause them psychological pain. For this reason, the term **psychedelic** ("mind manifesting" in Greek) is the more appropriate umbrella for these substances.

Within genre literature, "bad trips" may be the most common trope for psychedelic experience, where aspects of the tripper's mind or of the environment are twisted or magnified into terrifying monsters and dreamscapes. The awakening of psychic powers is another common trope, where healing experiences of wholeness and ego dissolution are conspicuously under-represented. The opposite is true in the medical literature, which has emphasized "the mystical experience," in which the tripper feels elevated and expanded, so that previous anxieties lose their emotional hold.

An exception is "Belief Changes Associated with Psychedelic Use," recently published in *Journal of Psychopharmacology*. This article is by researchers Sandeep Nayak, Manvir Singh, and patriarch of the modern study of psychedelics, Roland Griffiths of Johns Hopkins University, who regularly appears in documentaries and television shows. Unlike the researchers-turned-gurus of the 1960s, Timothy Leary and Ram Dass, who touted the potential of psychedelics to transform society, upending social conventions and religious traditions, Griffiths has scrupulously maintained a calm professional demeanor in his many public appearances, contributing to an atmosphere of hopeful caution around substances that so concerned the government during the Vietnam era that they were declared "public enemy number one" by then-President Richard Nixon.

Nayak, Singh, & Griffiths (2022) surveyed over two thousand people who reported significant belief changes after a single psychedelic experience, many of which were stable for an average of over **eight years**. They asked participants about their agreement with 45 statements covering a range of beliefs, which they collapsed into five categories through a mathematical technique called factor analysis, commonly used by social scientists in various disciplines.

- *Dualism,* or the separation of mind and body, including the ability of the mind to survive death of the body (ghosts and hauntings were not specifically addressed);
- *Paranormal/Spirituality,* or belief in psychic powers and magic;
- *Non-mammal consciousness,* encompassing "lower" animals and inanimate objects;
- *Mammal consciousness,* including "lower" mammals as well as our close relatives like apes and monkeys; and
- *Superstitions* such as bad luck.

Oddly, beliefs about the existence of cryptozoological creatures such as the Abominable Snowman and the Loch Ness Monster did not fit into any of these categories, and were more or less unaffected by a single psychedelic experience. Likewise, superstitious beliefs were rather rare and remained so after a single "trip." Conspiracy beliefs were not addressed in this study. However, **all** of the other categories in the survey increased significantly after a single psychedelic experience.

What this might mean for interest in and acceptance of paranormal ideas on a larger societal scale, once these drugs are in common psychiatric and therapeutic use, is unclear. Many of the respondents in this study were undoubtedly recreational users, who may have been predisposed to similar beliefs. Also, these subjects were mostly from the USA, Canada, and western Europe, which share a common cultural background that discounts paranormal experiences. Non-western cultures might have higher levels of belief to begin with, and might show different effects of exposure to psychedelics.

This study has nothing to say about the socially contagious aspects of belief, which would undoubtedly modify the effects of these drugs. In clinical studies they are almost always taken in a calm, quiet room, with one or even two sober counselors available to talk the tripper down should it be necessary, should the tripper become anxious and lose control, or otherwise become overwhelmed by the intensity of the experience. Many "bad trips" in a recreational setting are due to the contagious social influence of other intoxicated group members.

For further detailed examination, the categories of *Dualism* and *Paranormal/Spiritual* from Table 1 of Nayek, Singh, and Griffiths (2022) are reproduced below in Figures 1 and 2.

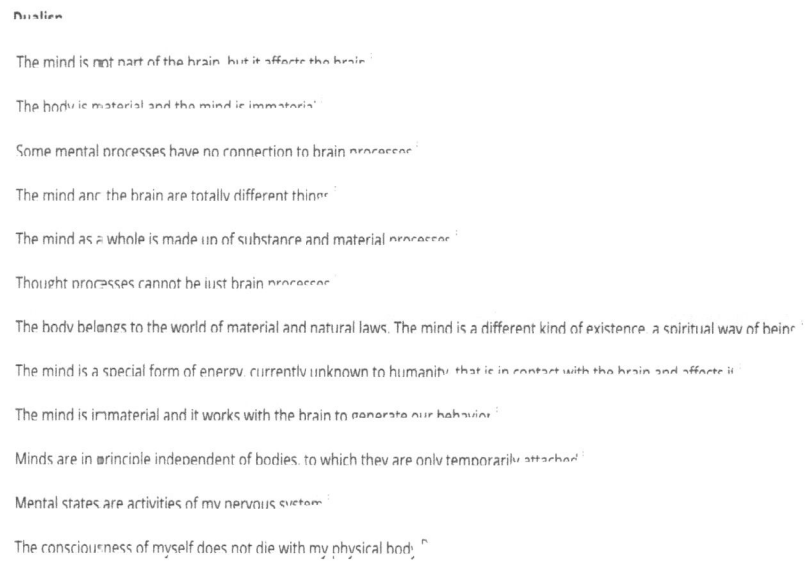

Dualism

The mind is not part of the brain, but it affects the brain.

The body is material and the mind is immaterial.

Some mental processes have no connection to brain processes.

The mind and the brain are totally different things.

The mind as a whole is made up of substance and material processes.

Thought processes cannot be just brain processes.

The body belongs to the world of material and natural laws. The mind is a different kind of existence, a spiritual way of being.

The mind is a special form of energy, currently unknown to humanity, that is in contact with the brain and affects it.

The mind is immaterial and it works with the brain to generate our behavior.

Minds are in principle independent of bodies, to which they are only temporarily attached.

Mental states are activities of my nervous system.

The consciousness of myself does not die with my physical body.

Figure 1. *Statements presented to psychedelic users. Agreement with all statements increased after psychedelic use. Percentages of before, after (one month), and current belief are available in the original paper, linked in the References below.*

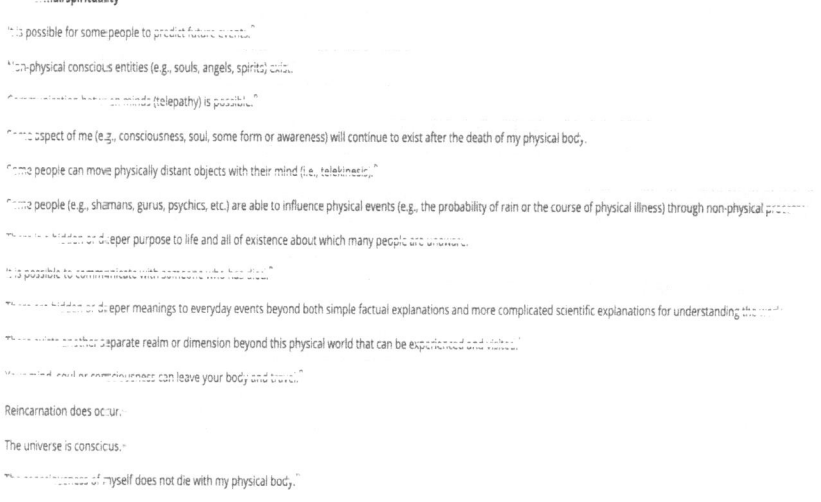

Paranormal/spirituality

It is possible for some people to predict future events.

Non-physical conscious entities (e.g., souls, angels, spirits) exist.

Communication between minds (telepathy) is possible.

Some aspect of me (e.g., consciousness, soul, some form or awareness) will continue to exist after the death of my physical body.

Some people can move physically distant objects with their mind (i.e., telekinesis).

Some people (e.g., shamans, gurus, psychics, etc.) are able to influence physical events (e.g., the probability of rain or the course of physical illness) through non-physical processes.

There is a hidden or deeper purpose to life and all of existence about which many people are unaware.

It is possible to communicate with someone who has died.

There are hidden or deeper meanings to everyday events beyond both simple factual explanations and more complicated scientific explanations for understanding the world.

There exists another separate realm or dimension beyond this physical world that can be experienced and visited.

Your mind, soul or consciousness can leave your body and travel.

Reincarnation does occur.

The universe is conscious.

The consciousness of myself does not die with my physical body.

Figure 2. *More statements presented to psychedelic users. Note that some statements (survival of death, etc.) are correlated with more than one category of belief. Percentages of increase and further details of experimental methods are available in the original paper.*

Note that, like most psychological researchers, this team asked about cognitive beliefs and not sensory experiences. This is in contrast to the subject of a previous *ParABnormal* article, Tanya Luhrman, who studies immediate and remembered religious and spiritual experiences directly. However, her underlying model, of a porous imagined boundary between the mind and the world, has much in common with the statements presented to the subjects of this study (Luhrman & Weisman, 2022). Her work has the additional virtue of engaging with various cultures around the world. A more recent paper emphasizes the diversity of ideas about this boundary, even within the same individuals, under different circumstances:

> we argue that all humans have conflicting intuitions about the relationship between inner experience and outer world ... We suggest that different local social worlds offer people different invitations to attend to, interpret, and resolve these conflicting intuitions, so that people in some settings, compared with others, more confidently assert [paranormal beliefs].

In other words, just as "set and setting" are known to modify psychedelic drug experiences, they also modify experience under other, more mundane circumstances.

Western cultures have used either/or thinking and the process of elimination to great effect over the past several centuries, but it may be time to adopt a more both/and style of thinking, especially where the mind is concerned.

REFERENCES / FURTHER READING

MacBride, K.(2022). "I Am Certain That the LSD Experience Has Helped Me Very Much." *Inverse.*
https://www.inverse.com/mind-body/alcoholics-anonymous-lsd-bill-wilson

Nayak, S.M., Singh, M., & Griffiths, R.R. (2022). Belief changes associated with psychedelic use. *Journal of Psychopharmacology*, 37(1):80-92.
https://journals.sagepub.com/doi/10.1177/0 2698811221131989

Luhrmann, T. M., & Weisman, K. (2022). Porosity Is the Heart of Religion. *Current Directions in Psychological Science*, 31(3), 247–253.
https://doi.org/10.1177/09637214221075285
https://www.academia.edu/92800646/Porosit y_Is_the_Heart_of_Religion

Printed in the USA
CPSIA information can be obtained
at www.ICGtesting.com
LVHW020801290923
759457LV00019B/969

9 781088 273074